# THIS LITTLE PIGGY

## AN OWNER'S MANUAL

by Cyndi Marko

### ALADDIN

New York   London   Toronto   Sydney   New Delhi

# ALADDIN

An imprint of Simon & Schuster Children's Publishing Division
1230 Avenue of the Americas, New York, New York 10020
This Aladdin edition March 2021
Copyright © 2017 by Cyndi Marko
All rights reserved, including the right of reproduction in whole or in part in any form.
ALADDIN and related logo are registered trademarks of Simon & Schuster, Inc.
For information about special discounts for bulk purchases, please contact
Simon & Schuster Special Sales at 1-866-506-1949 or business@simonandschuster.com.
The Simon & Schuster Speakers Bureau can bring authors to your live event. For more information
or to book an event contact the Simon & Schuster Speakers Bureau at 1-866-248-3049
or visit our website at www.simonspeakers.com.
Designed by Laura Lyn DiSiena
The illustrations for this book were rendered in colored pencil, watercolor, and ink.
The text of this book was set in MetallophileSP8.
Manufactured in China 0121 SCP
2 4 6 8 10 9 7 5 3 1
Library of Congress Control Number 2020937990
ISBN 978-1-5344-8109-1(hc)
ISBN 978-1-5344-8108-4 (pbk)
ISBN 978-1-4814-6827-5 (eBook)

For Mom, who grounded me for not liking her garden. And for Dad, who didn't let me have a puppy. You big meanies. (But I ♥ you.)

And ginormous thanks to my editor, Karen Nagel; my designer, Laura Lyn DiSiena; and my agent, Adriann Ranta, for their many contributions and their support in making Snowflake sparkle.

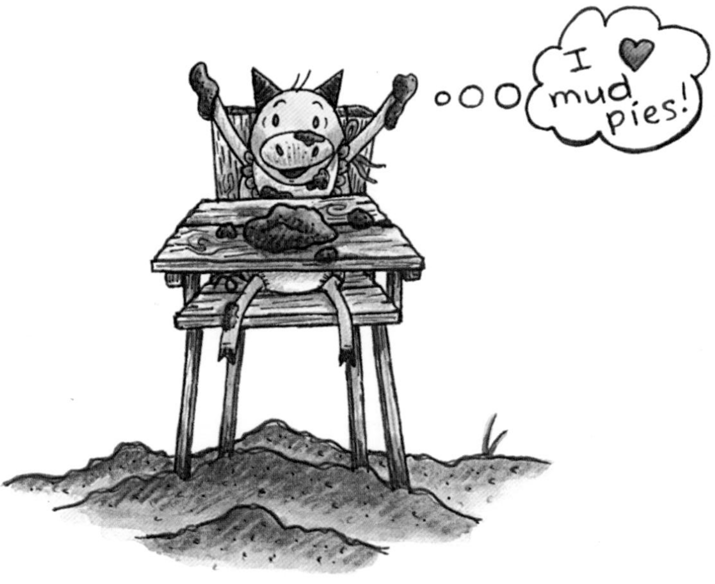
I ♥ mud pies!

# CHAPTER ONE

Have you always wanted a pet
with all your heart?

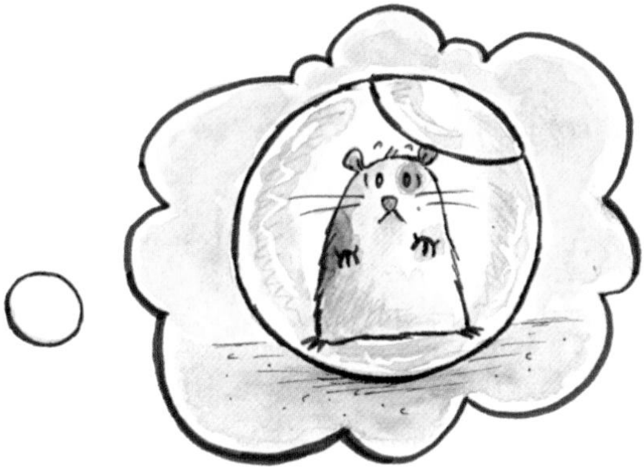

Cute ball of fur.

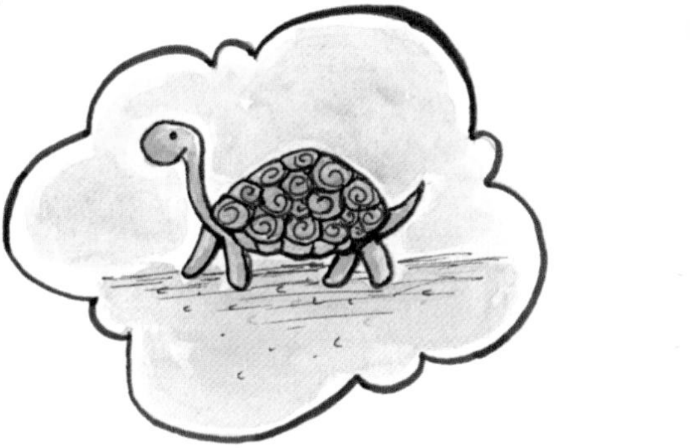

Slow and slimy.

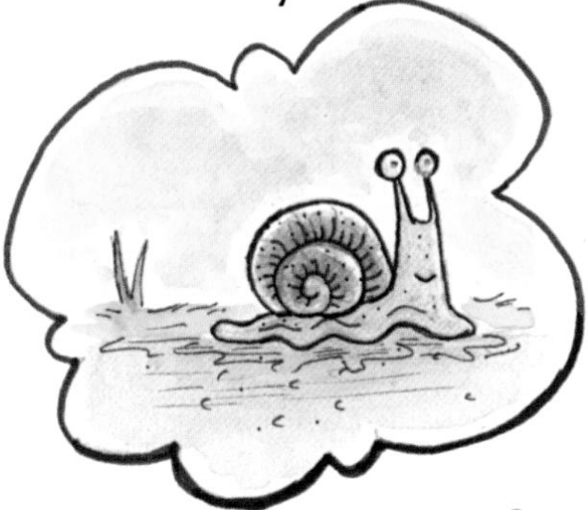

Comes with a house.

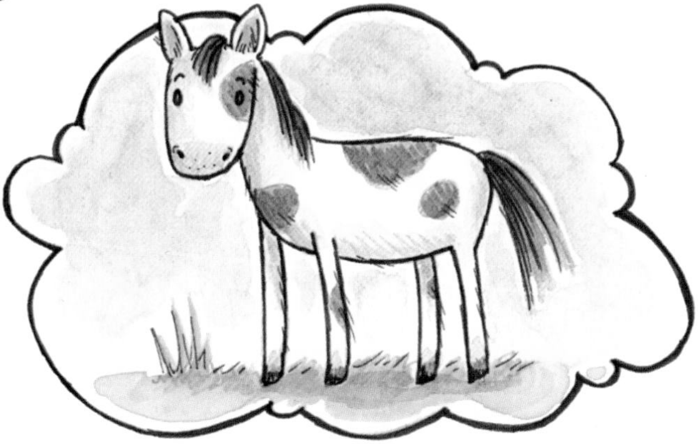

Giddyup!

It seems like everyone you know has a pet. Your friend Bowie's Saint Bernard rescues mountain climbers.

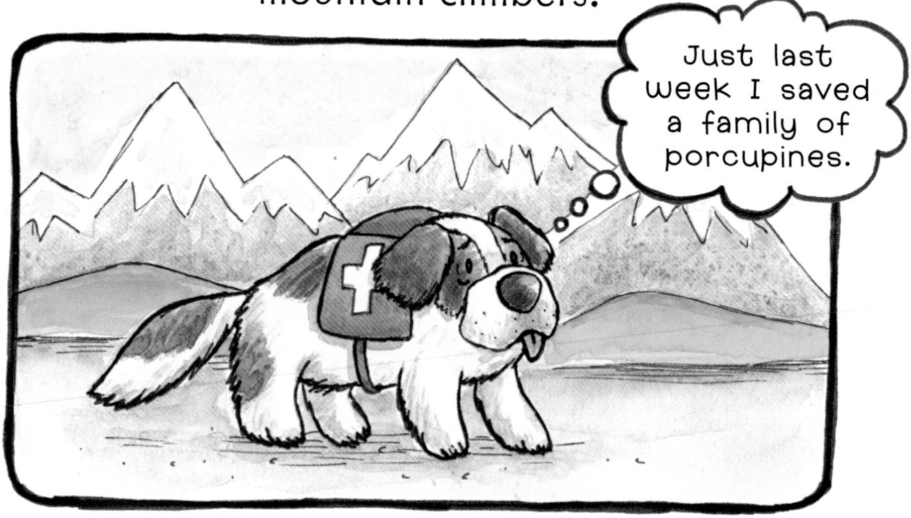
Just last week I saved a family of porcupines.

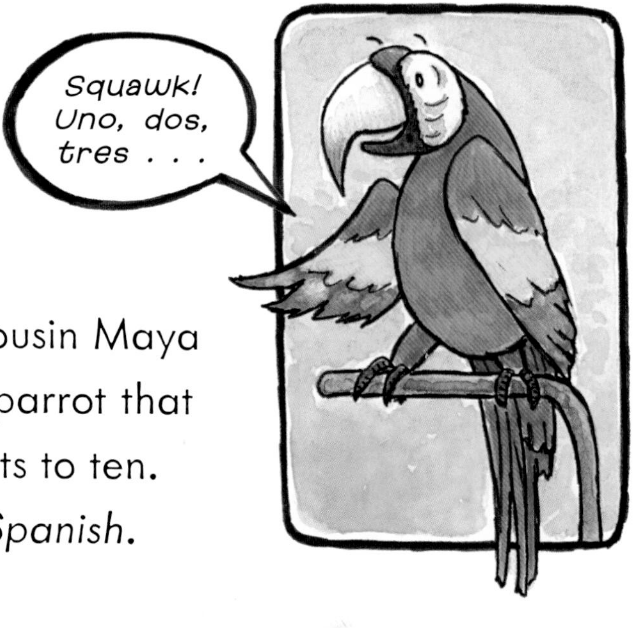
*Squawk! Uno, dos, tres . . .*

Your cousin Maya has a parrot that counts to ten. In *Spanish*.

And your neighbor Mr. Bumble's cool chameleon changes color from pink to turquoise.

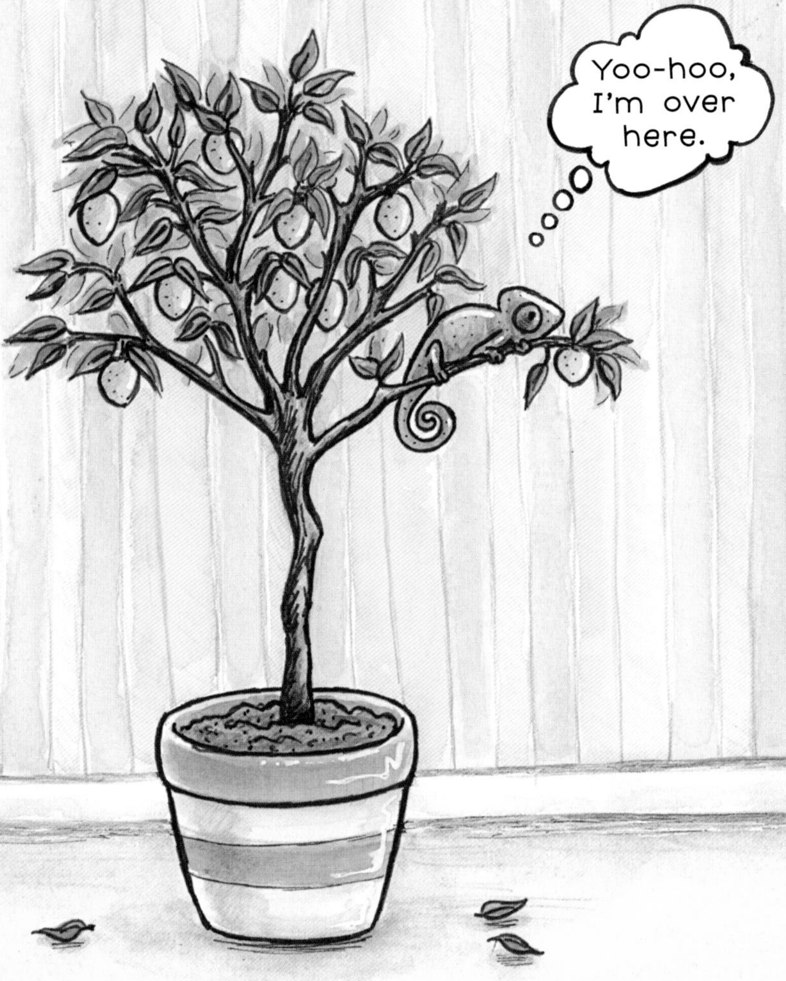
Yoo-hoo, I'm over here.

But I bet *you've* always wanted . . .

A PIG!

Pigs are AWESOME. They have:

a twitchy,
itchy snout,

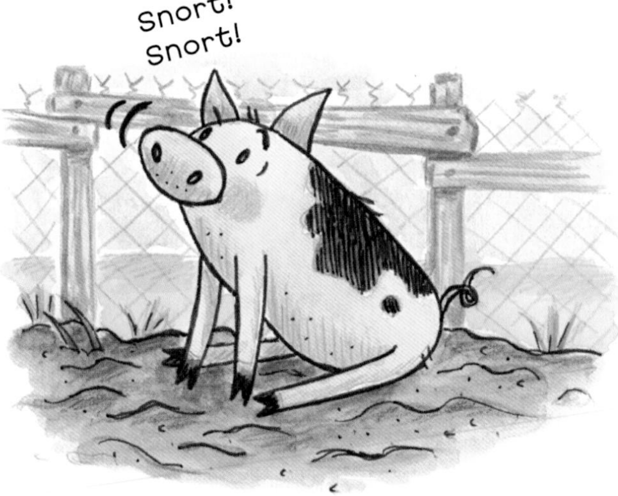
Snort!
Snort!

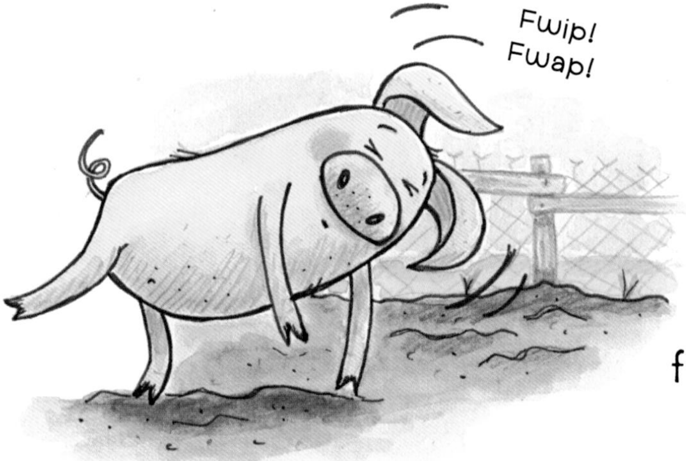
Fwip!
Fwap!

flippy,
flappy ears,
and

a springy,
sproingy tail.

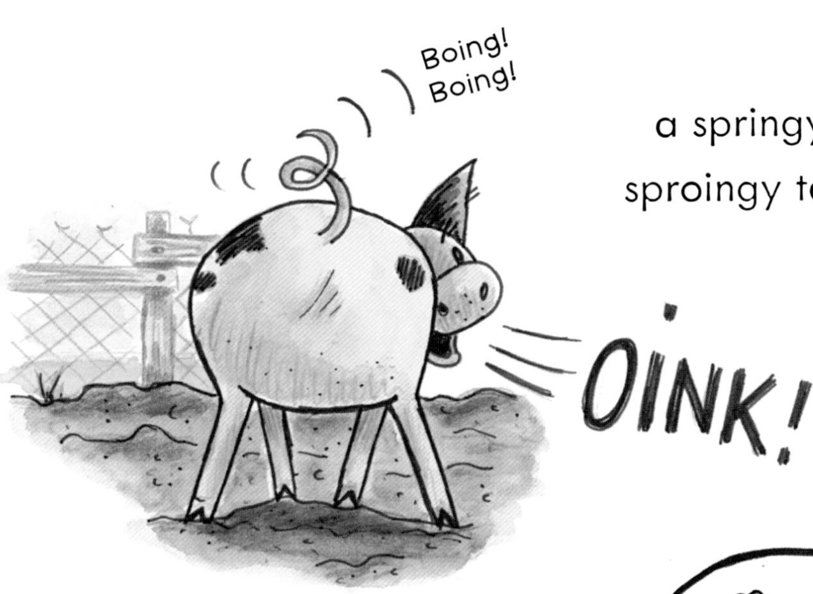
Boing!
Boing!
OINK!

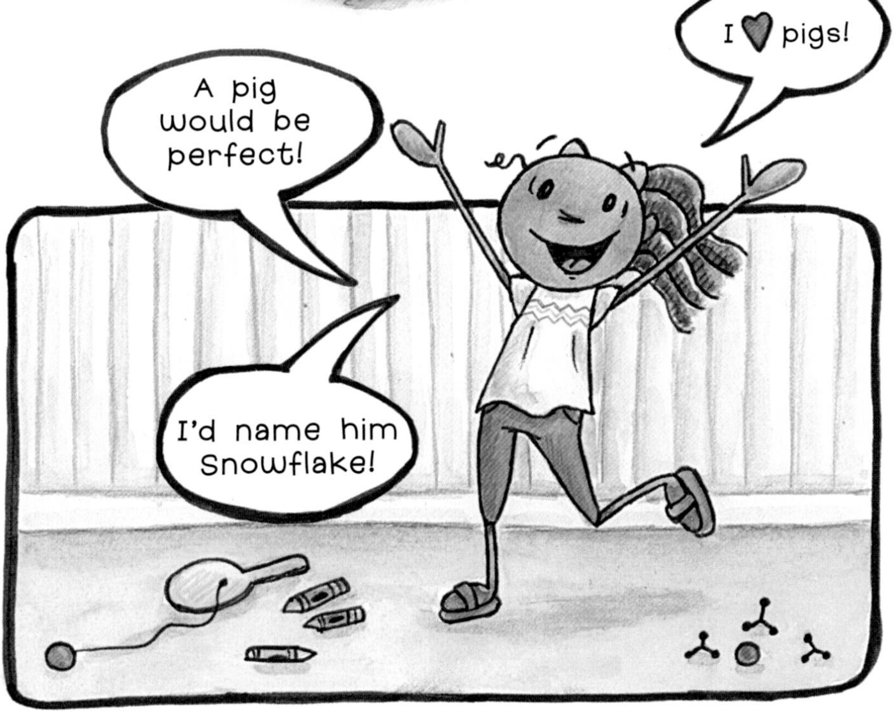
I ♥ pigs!
A pig would be perfect!
I'd name him Snowflake!

Of course, your brother might have other ideas. . . .

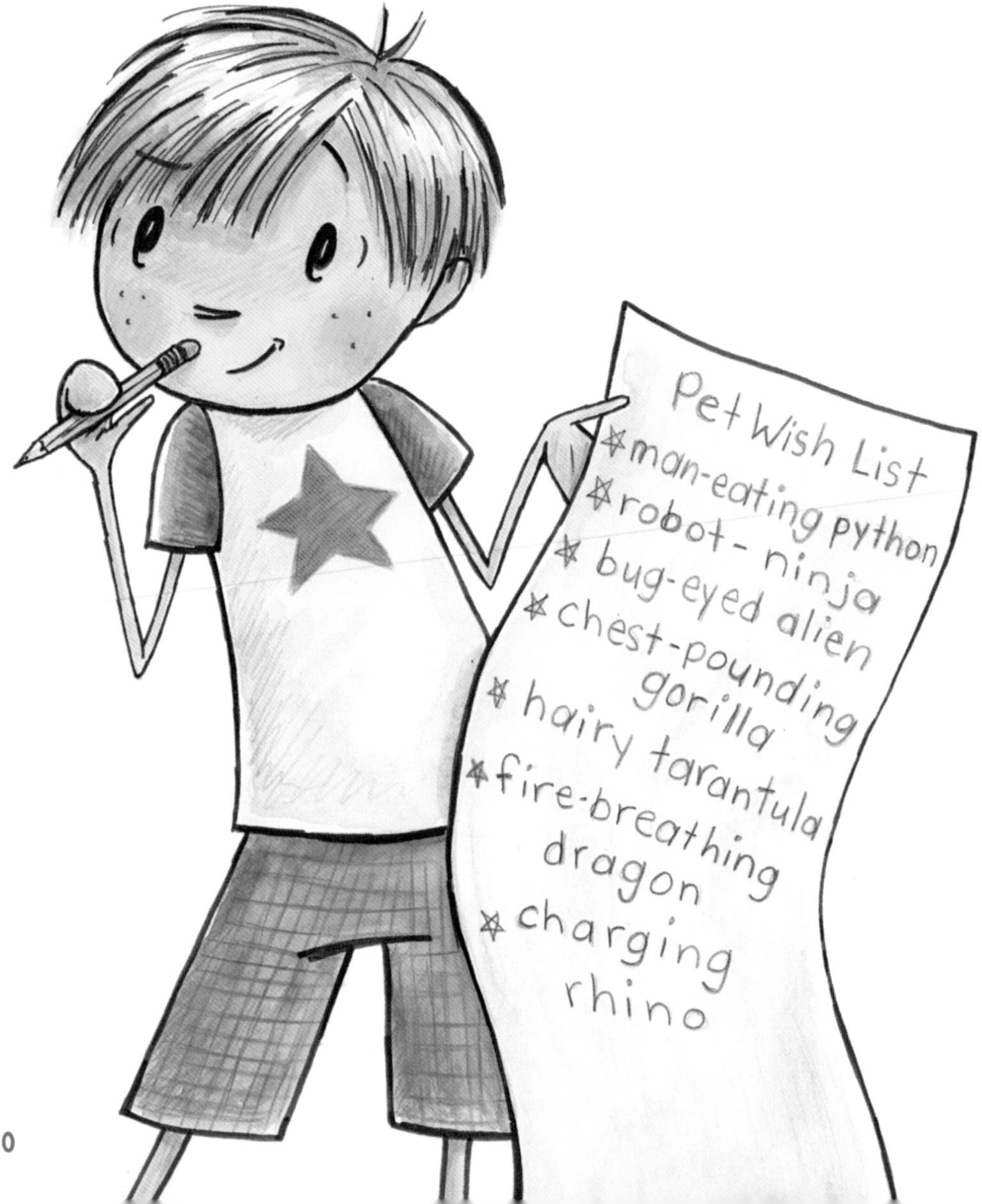
Pet Wish List
man-eating python
robot-ninja
bug-eyed alien
chest-pounding gorilla
hairy tarantula
fire-breathing dragon
charging rhino

You have to admit, a gorilla would be sort of neat. . . .

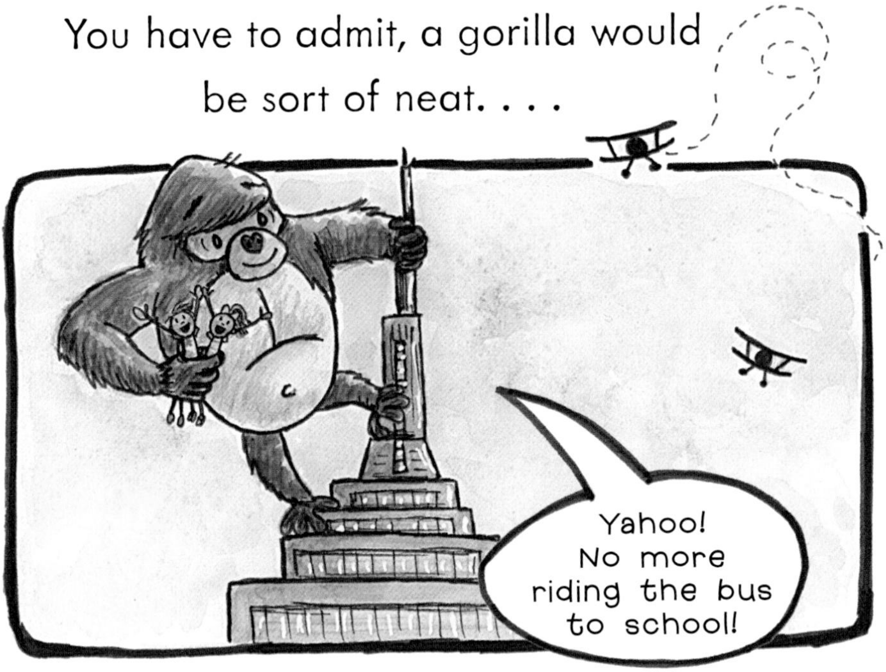
Yahoo!
No more riding the bus to school!

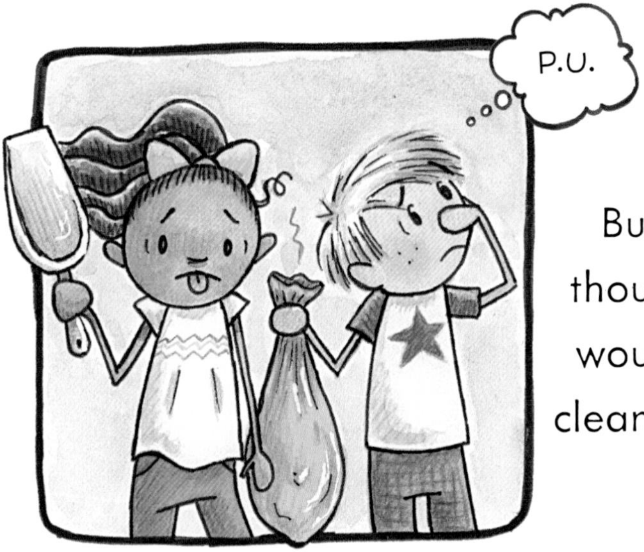
P.U.

But on second thought, you sure wouldn't want to clean up after him.

Your brother might not care that pigs are louder than motorcycles,

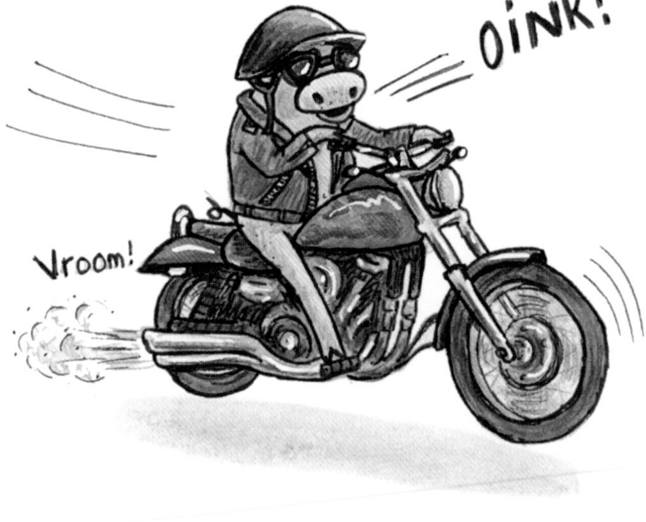
OINK!
Vroom!

have forty-four teeth (say "cheese"!),

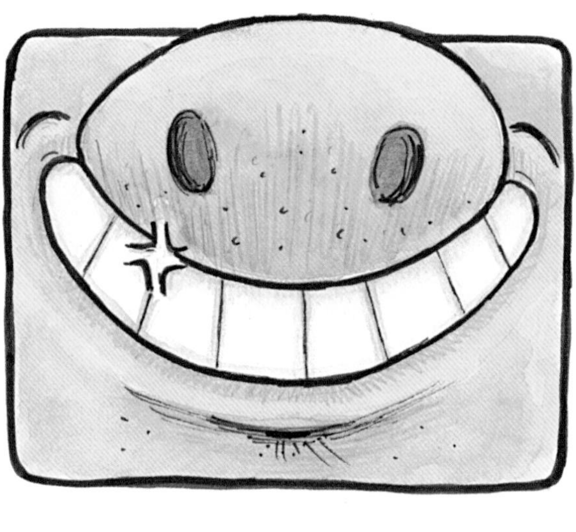

and live on every continent except Antarctica,

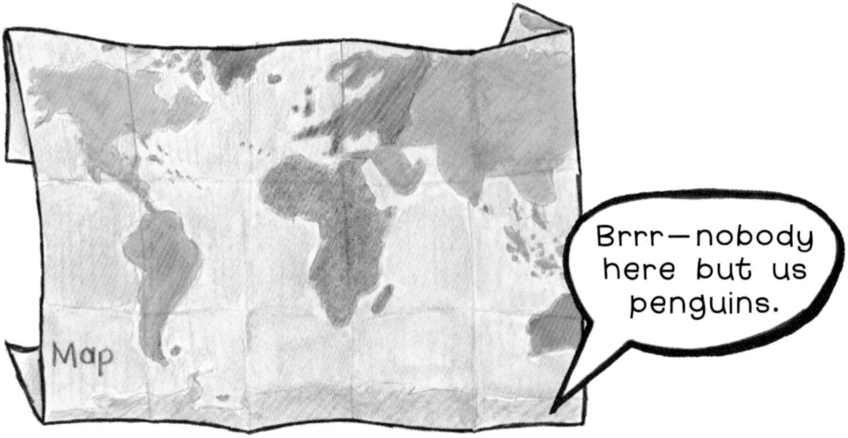
Map
Brrr—nobody here but us penguins.

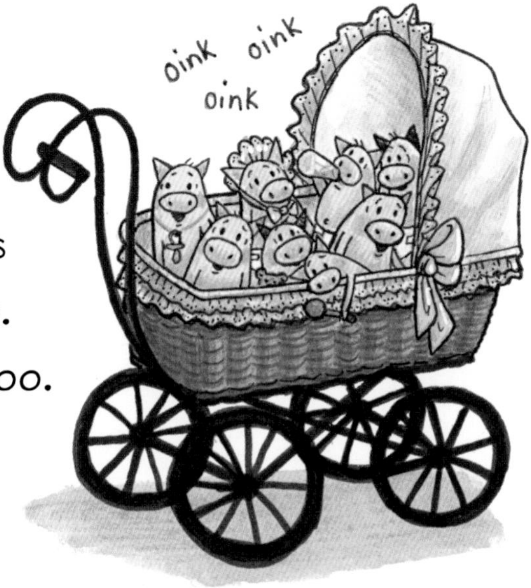
oink oink
oink

or that baby pigs
are called piglets.
*Coochie, coochie, coo.*

I know you can win him over!
Tell him that pigs . . .

love mud!

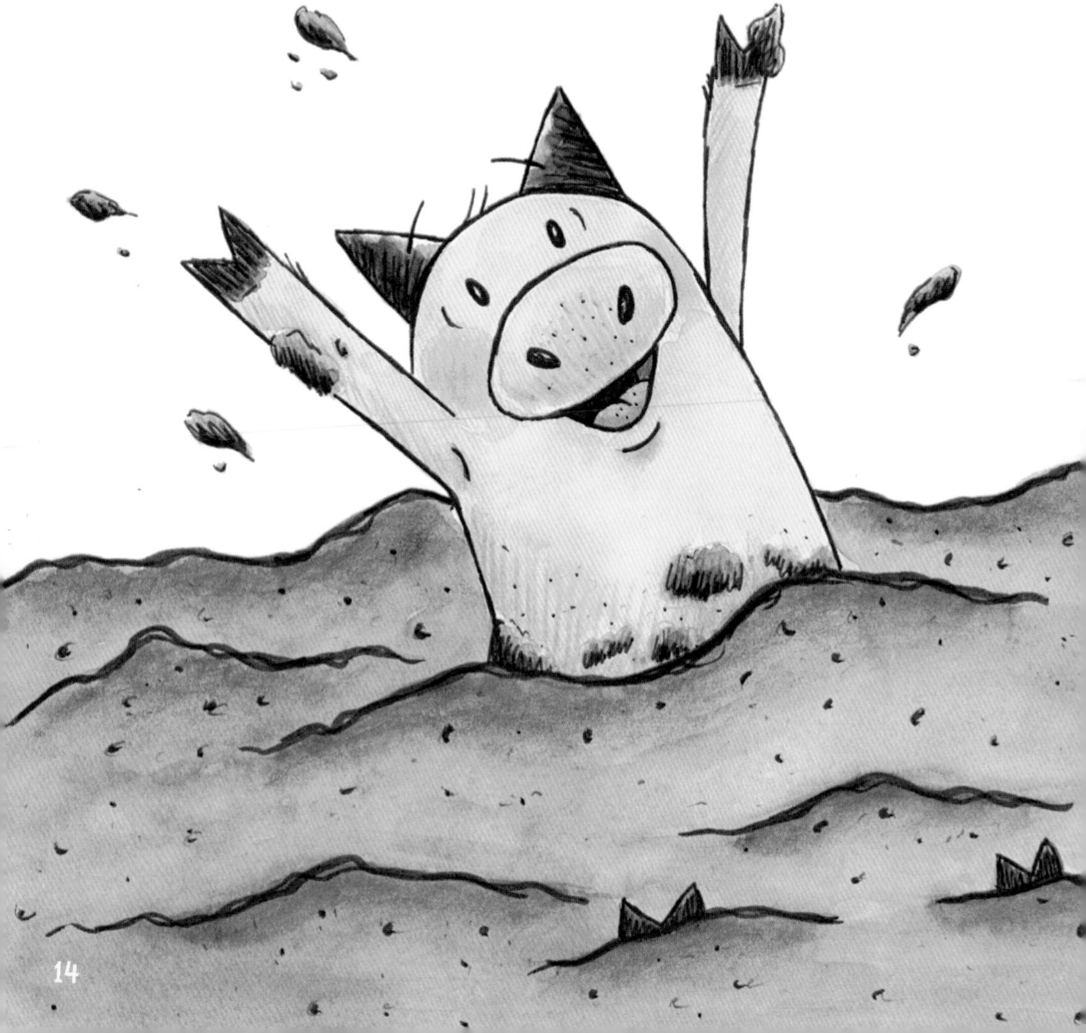

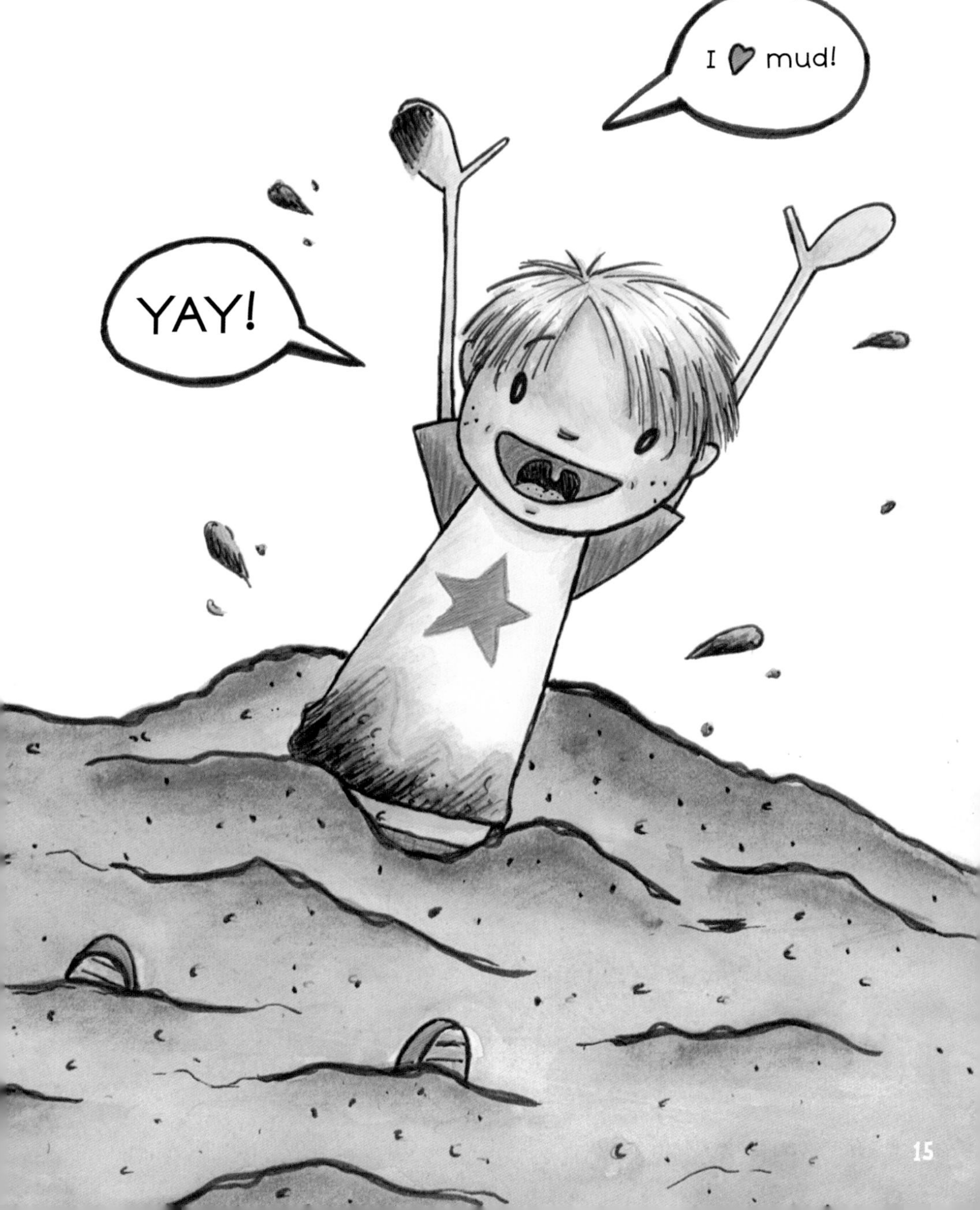
YAY!
I ♥ mud!

# CHAPTER TWO

Getting your brother on board the piggy train was the easy part.

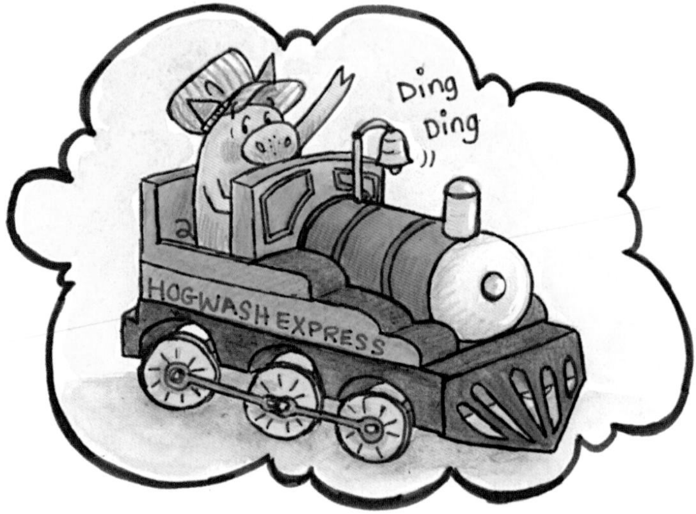
Ding
Ding
2
HOGWASH EXPRESS

Now you have to convince your mother that there is no better pet in the ENTIRE universe than a pig. There is just one small problem:

your mother's favorite pets are from the *garden*.

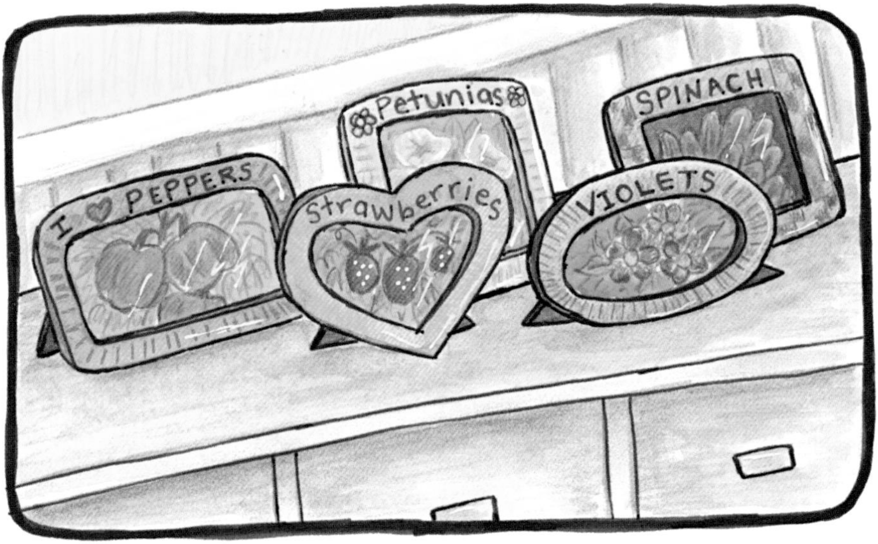
Petunias
SPINACH
I ♥ PEPPERS
Strawberries
VIOLETS

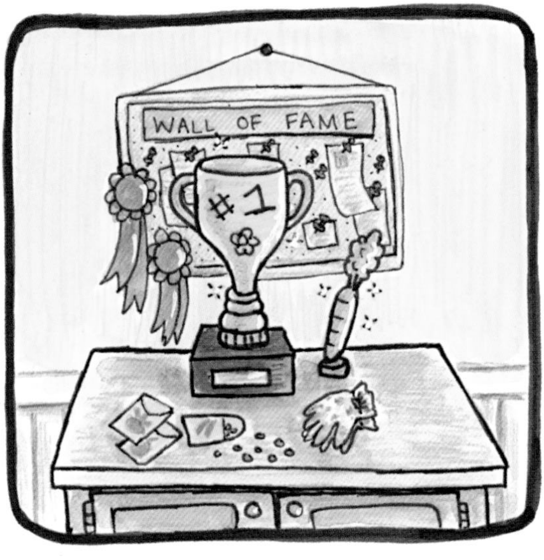
WALL OF FAME
#1

You are right that garden plants are not pets. But try telling your mother that.

Obviously, you have your work cut out for you. You'll need to hatch a scheme.

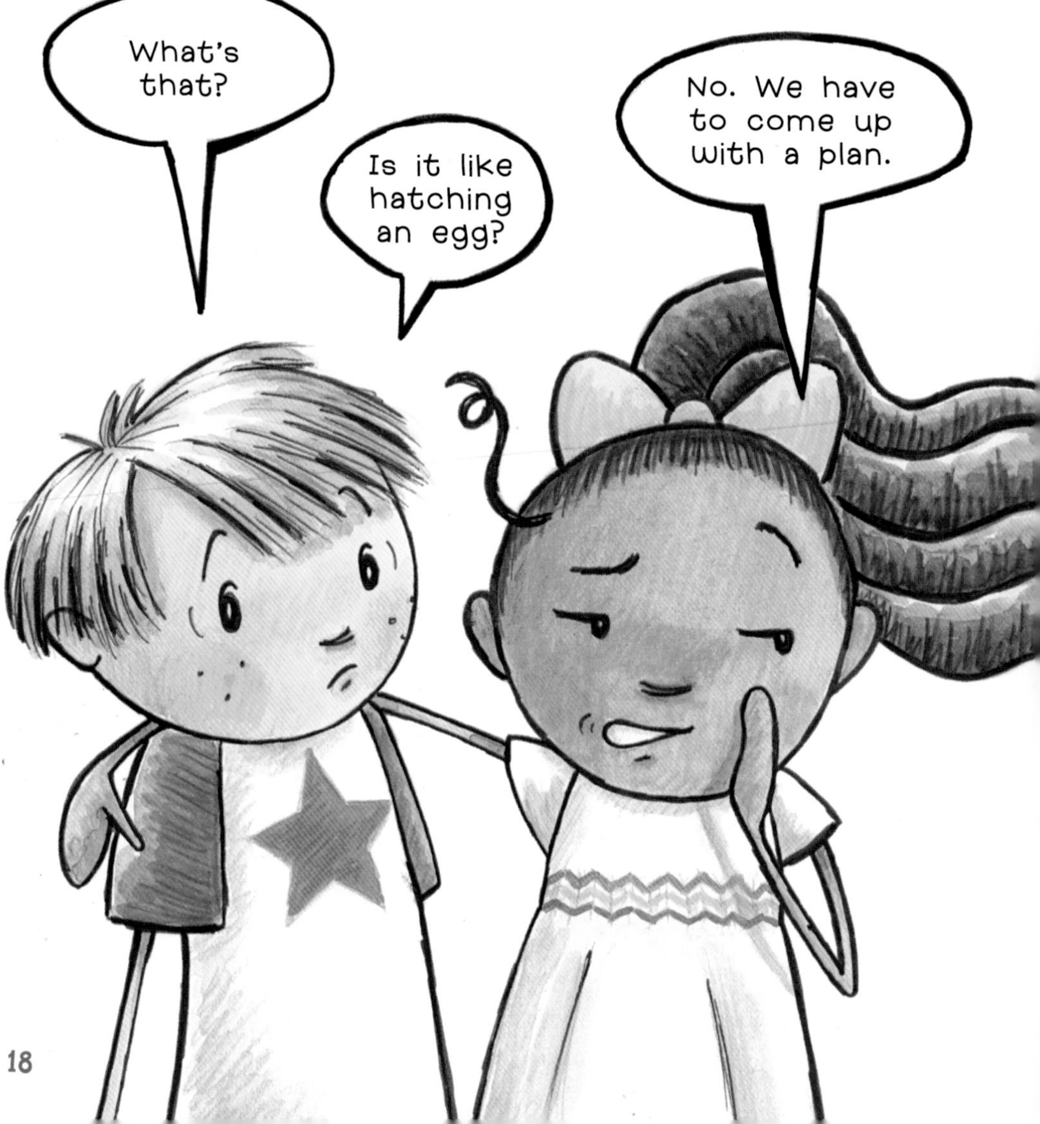
What's that?
Is it like hatching an egg?
No. We have to come up with a plan.

Remember when you
wanted to eat ice
cream for dinner?

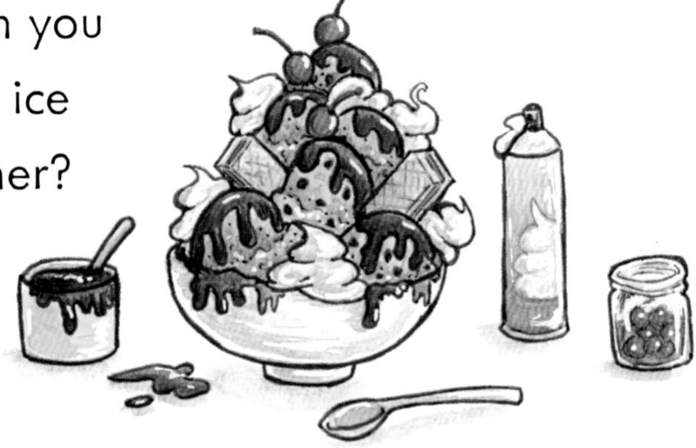

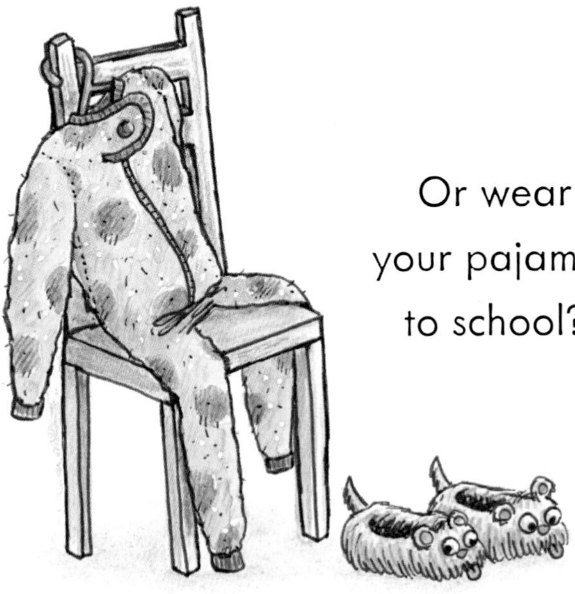

Or wear
your pajamas
to school?

And how you had to fool (I mean, convince)
your mom that those were great ideas?
And she fell for it (I mean, agreed)?

To get your scheme started, make a checklist. Lists are great for staying organized. And by the look of this pigsty, you need help in that department.

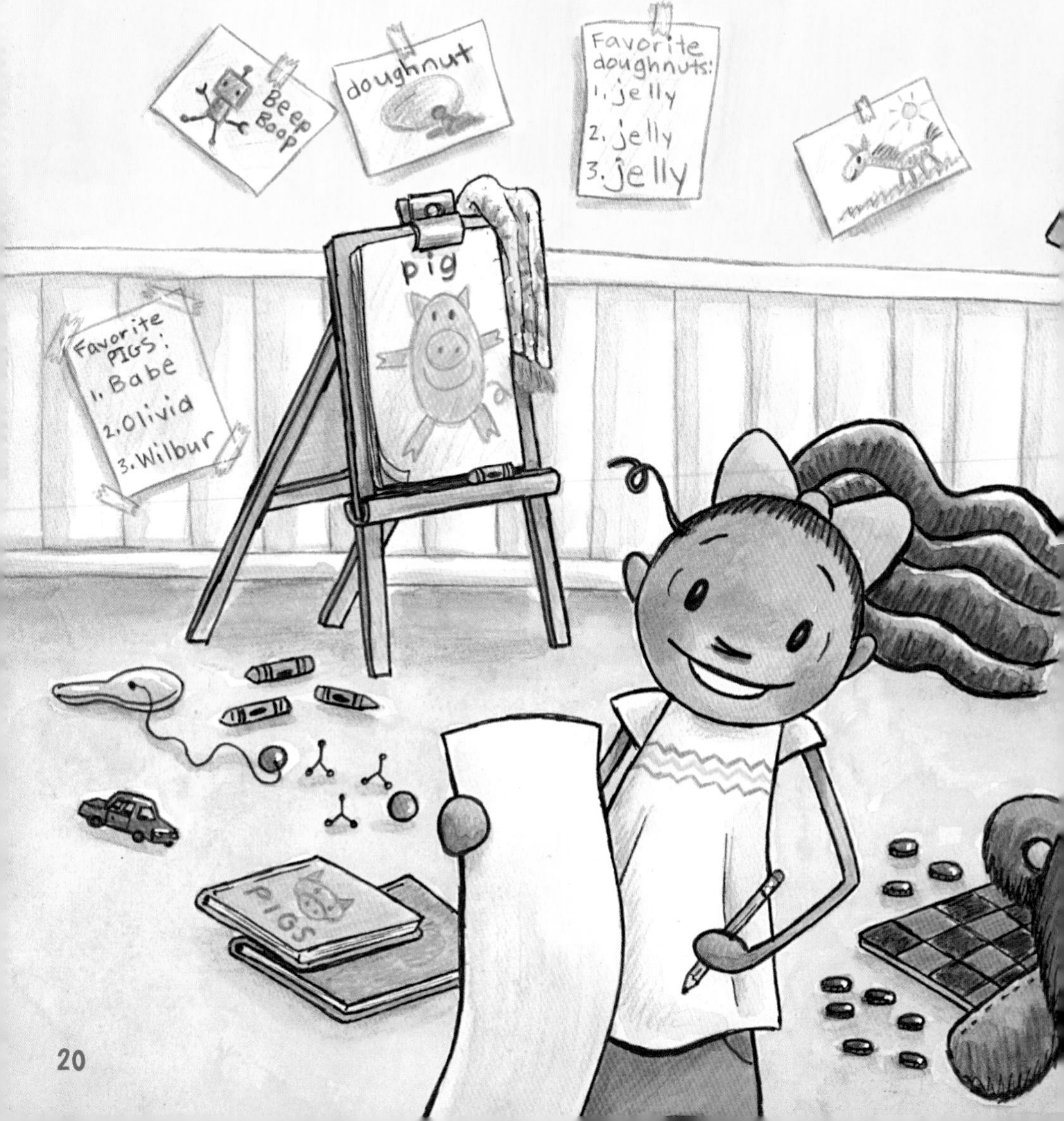
Beep Boop
doughnut
Favorite doughnuts:
1. jelly
2. jelly
3. jelly
pig
Favorite PIGS:
1. Babe
2. Olivia
3. Wilbur
PIGS

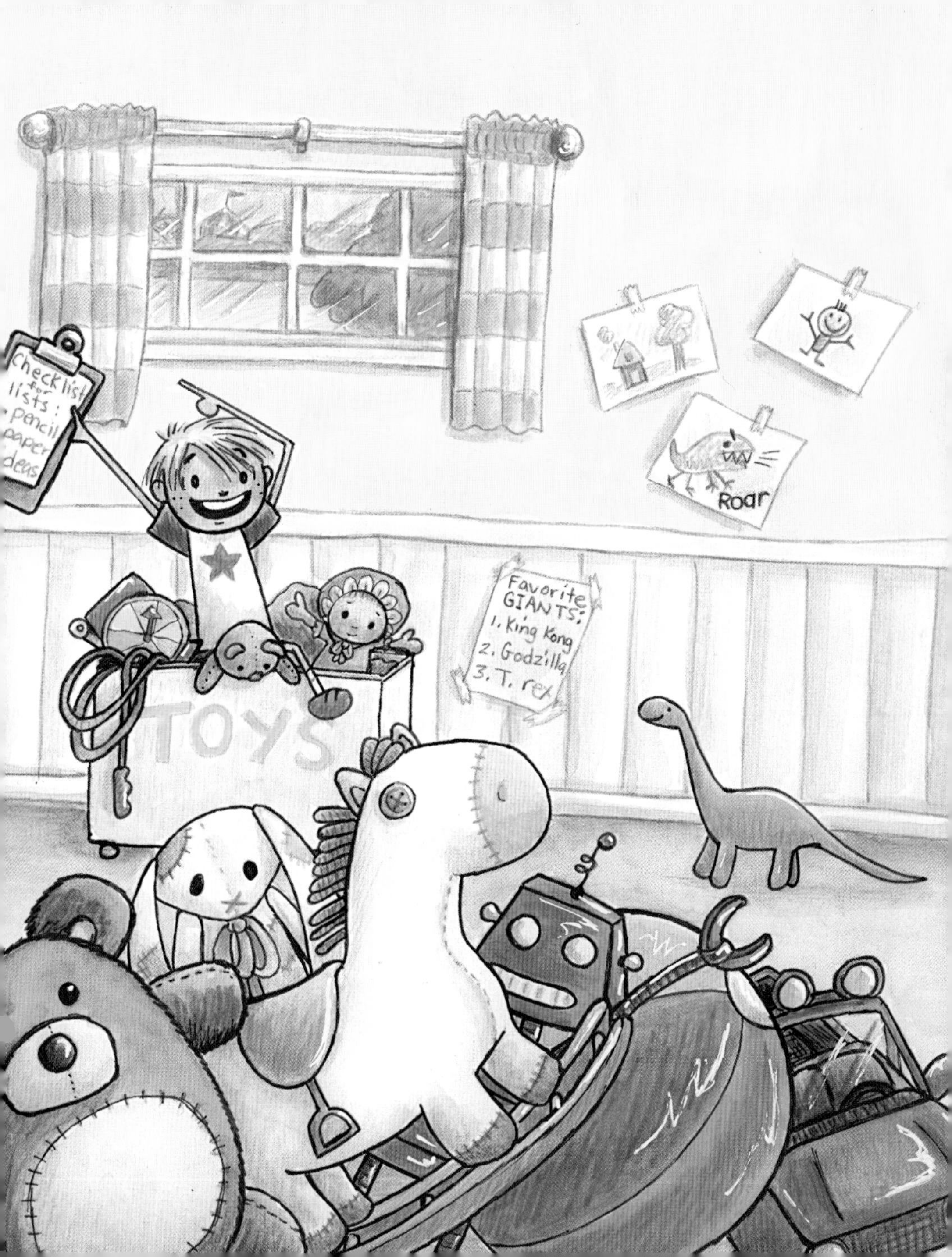

Checklist for lists: pencil paper ideas
Roar
Favorite GIANTS: 1. King Kong 2. Godzilla 3. T. rex
TOYS

First pick a pig.
Try to pick one with *potential*.

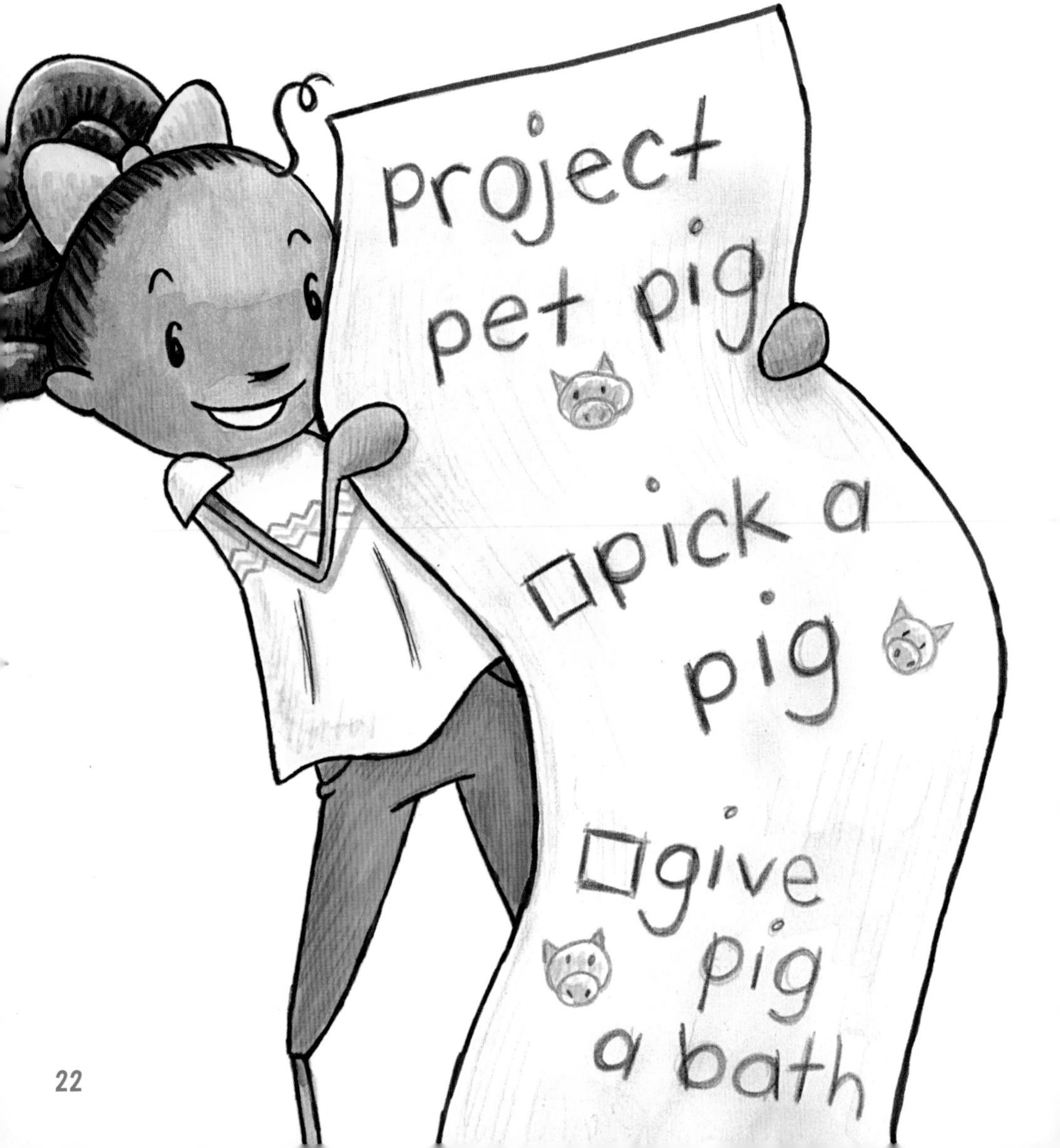
project
pet pig
□pick a
pig
□give
pig
a bath

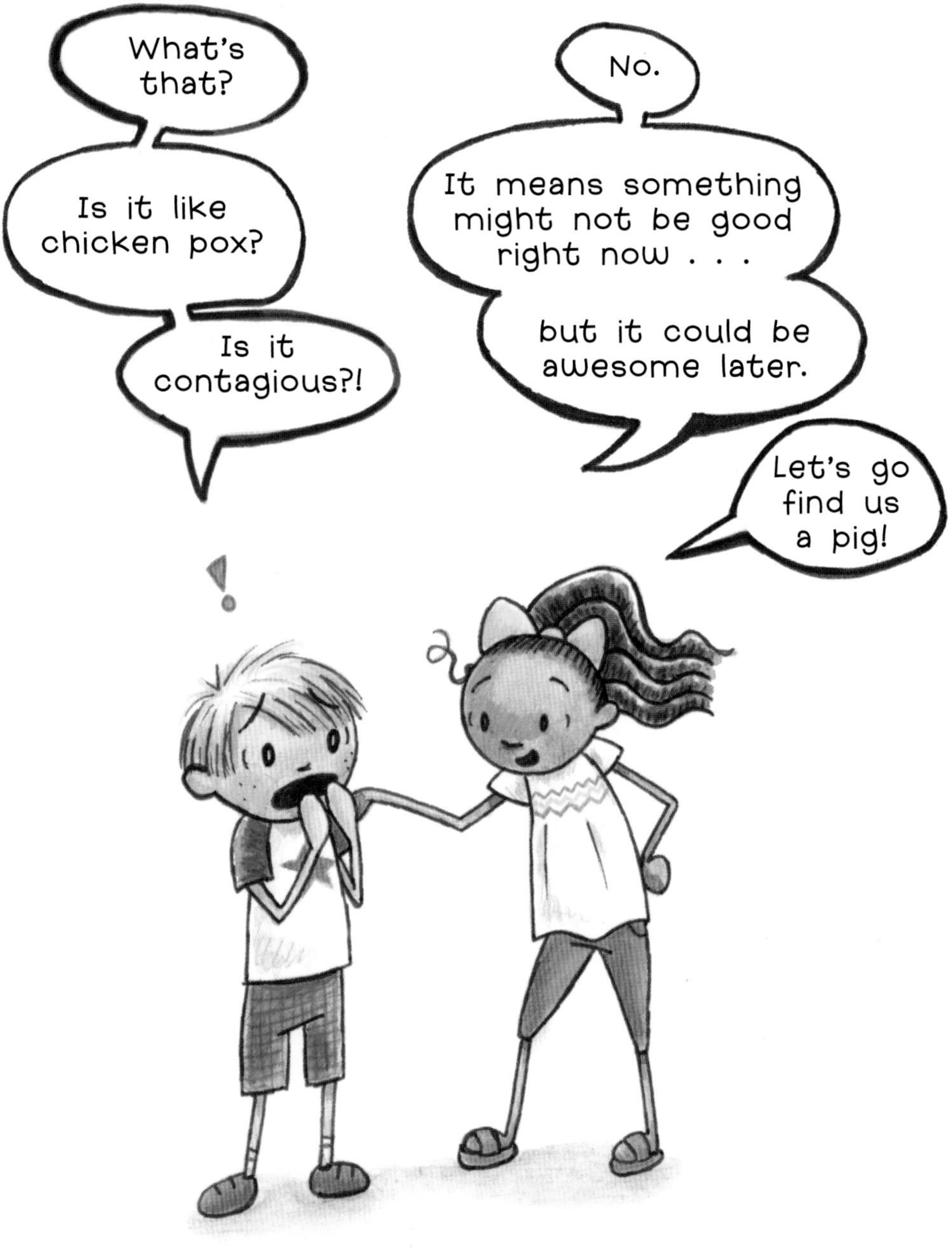
What's that?
Is it like chicken pox?
Is it contagious?!
No.
It means something might not be good right now . . .
but it could be awesome later.
Let's go find us a pig!

Amazingly, there's one—stuck in the mud.

He's your Snowflake.

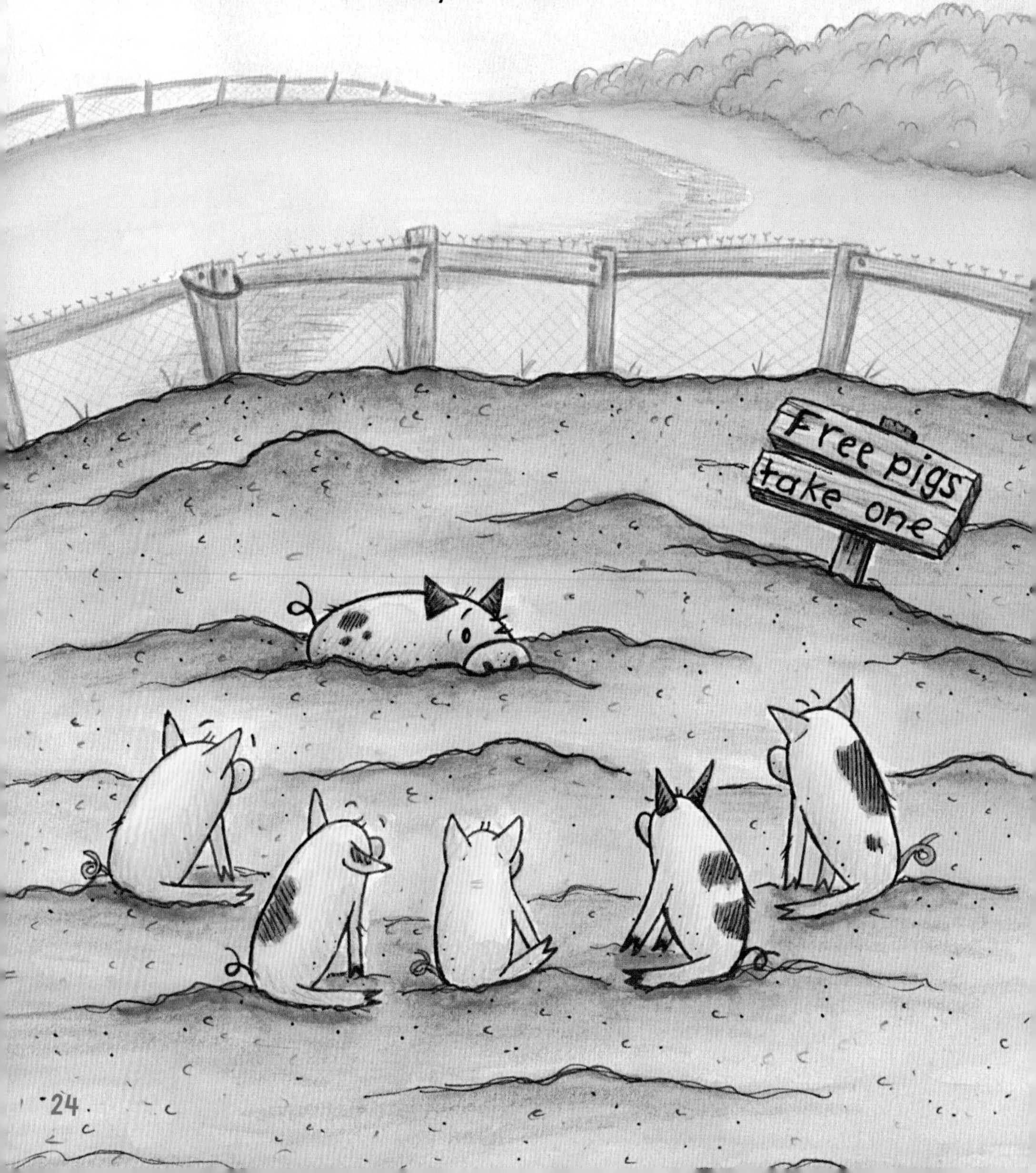
Free pigs
take one

# CHAPTER THREE

Now that you've picked your pig,
let's move on.
Your pig is *terrifically* dirty, and
your mother only likes dirt in the garden.
Time for a bath! You'll need:

☐ washtub

☐ soap
(extra sudsy)

☐ water
(H$_2$O)

Once the washtub is filled to the brim,
the bath is ready for your pig.

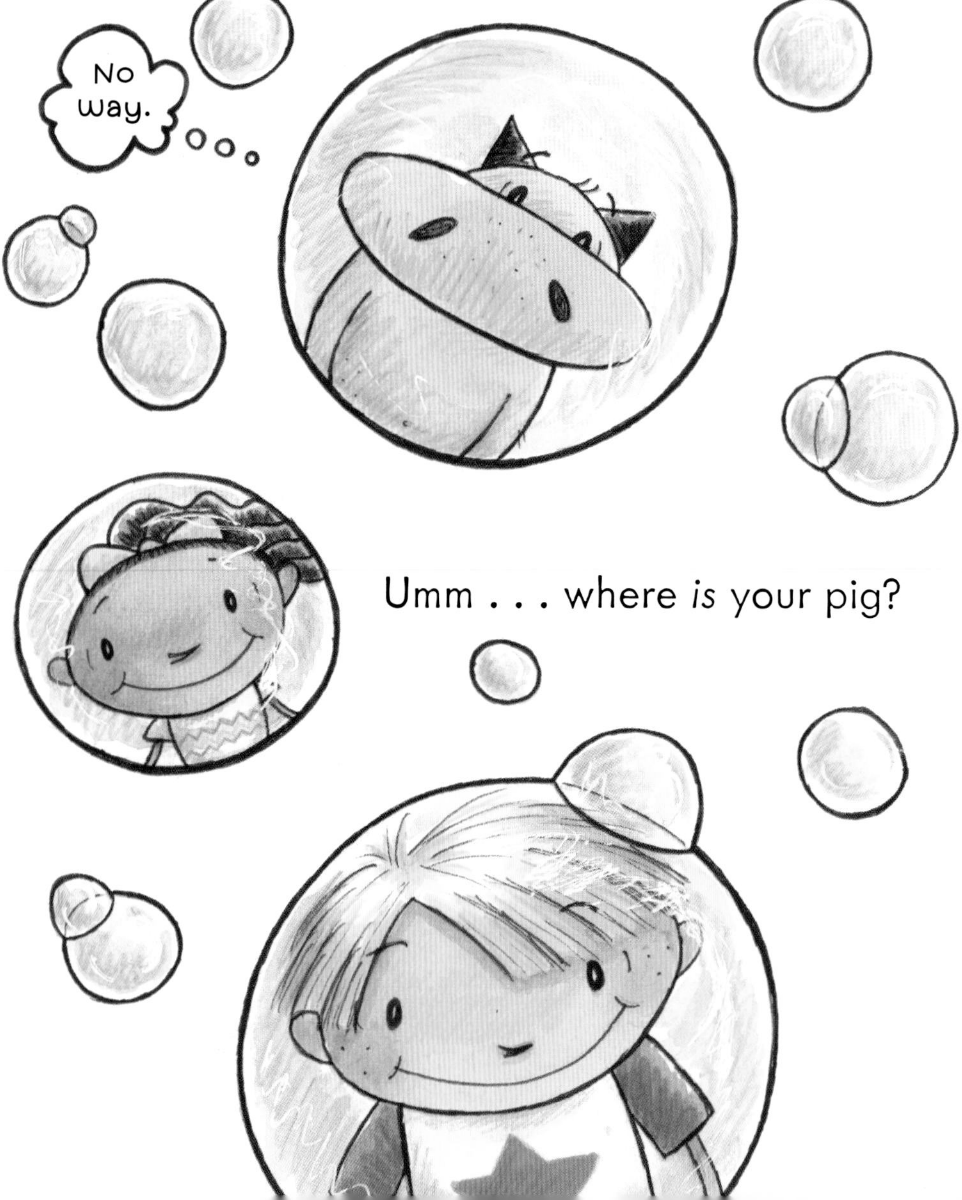
No way.

Umm . . . where *is* your pig?

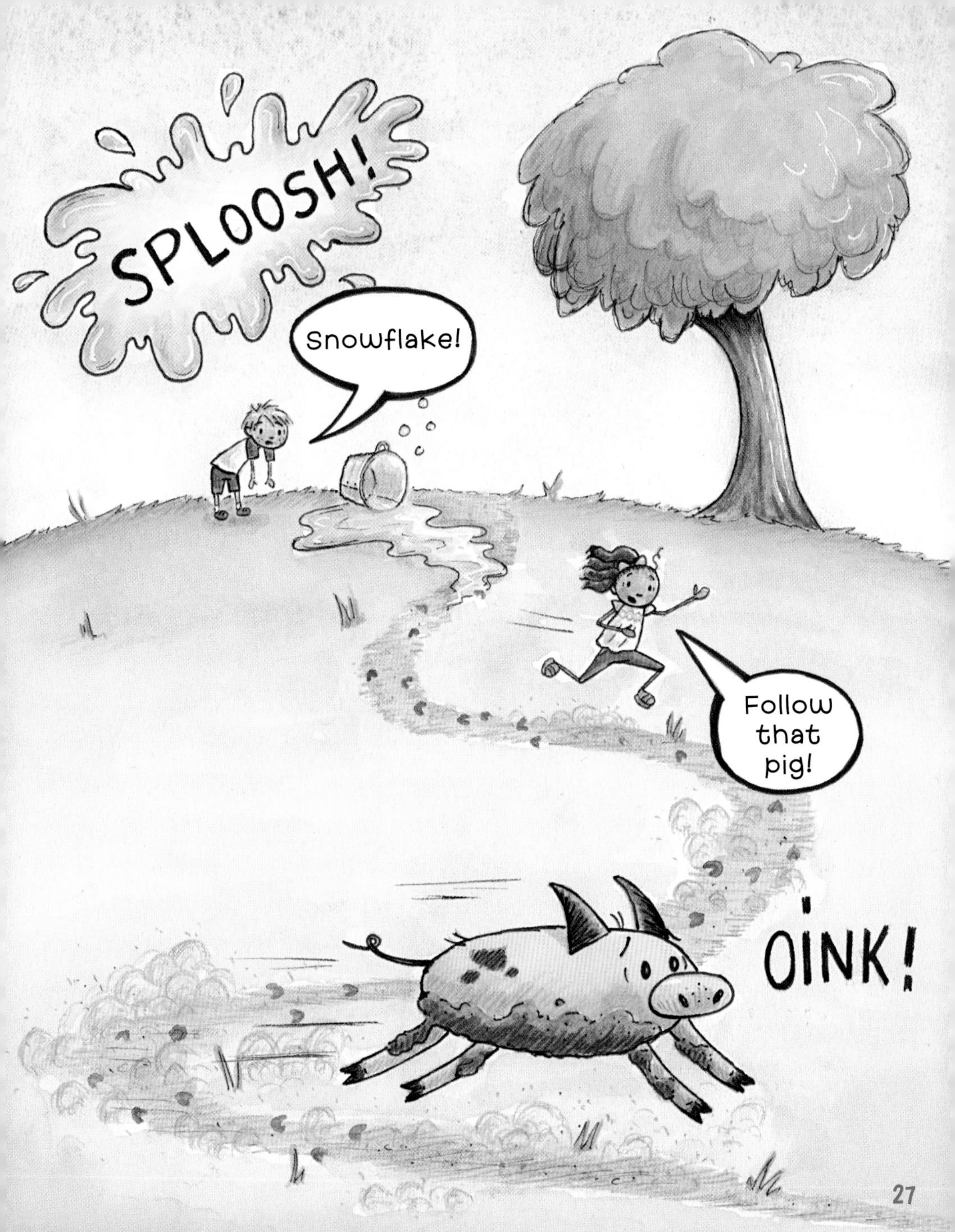
SPLOOSH!
Snowflake!
Follow that pig!
OINK!

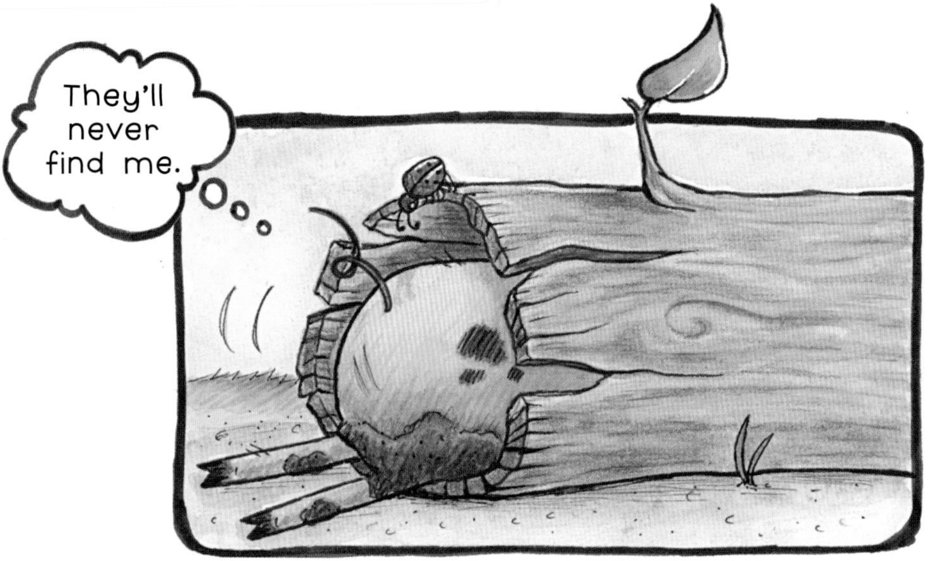
They'll never find me.

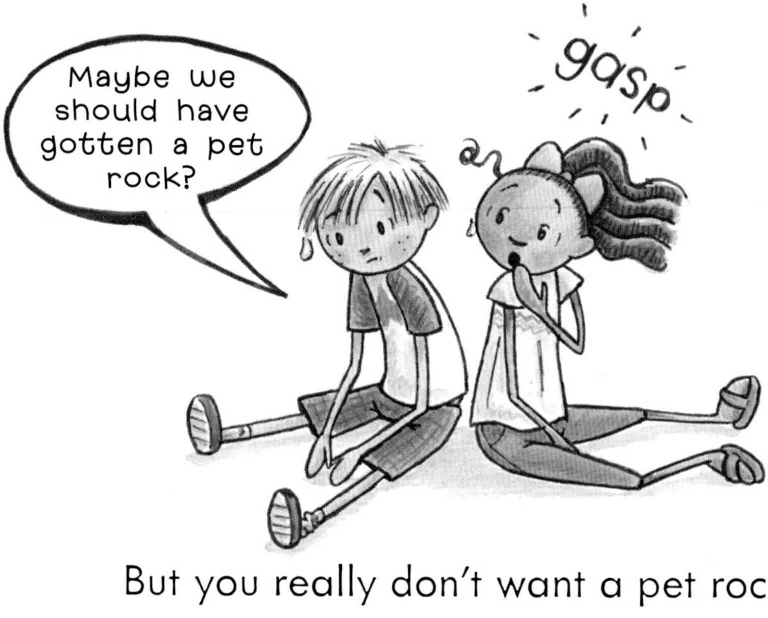
Maybe we should have gotten a pet rock?
gasp

But you really don't want a pet rock.
(And sometimes you're not sure
you really want a brother. . . .)

Back to bathing.
Refill the tub with
*warm* soapy water.

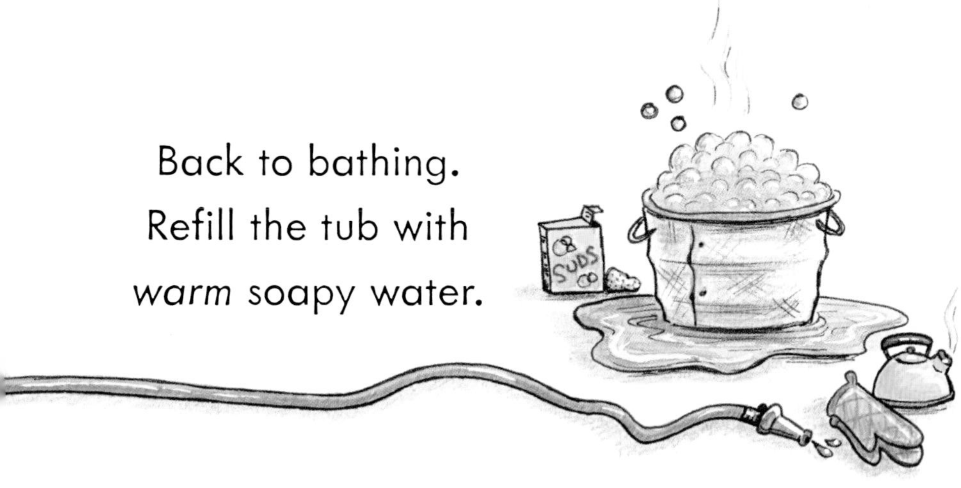
SUDS

Scrub your pig all over. Mom will love a clean pig as much as she does a red pepper.

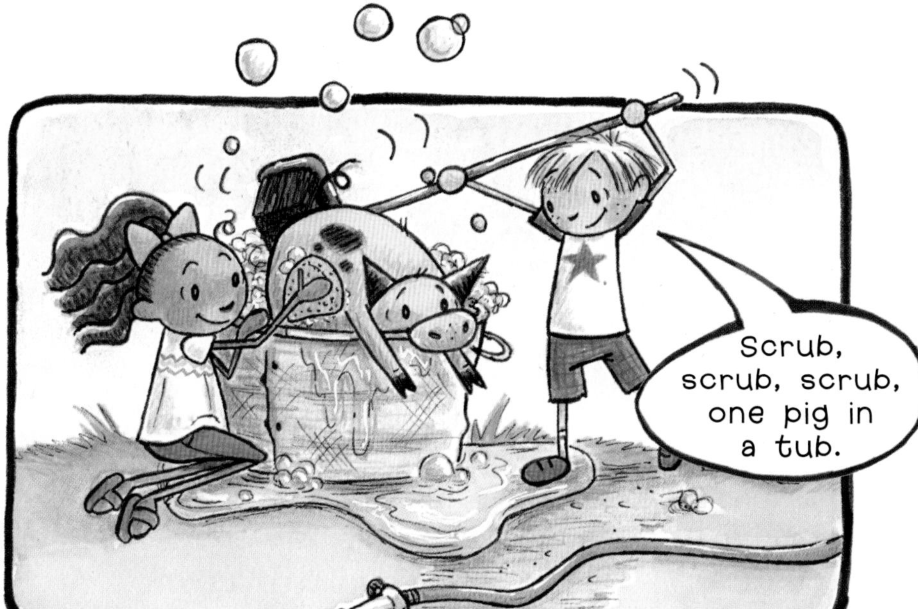
Scrub, scrub, scrub, one pig in a tub.

Next, dry your pig with a soft towel.

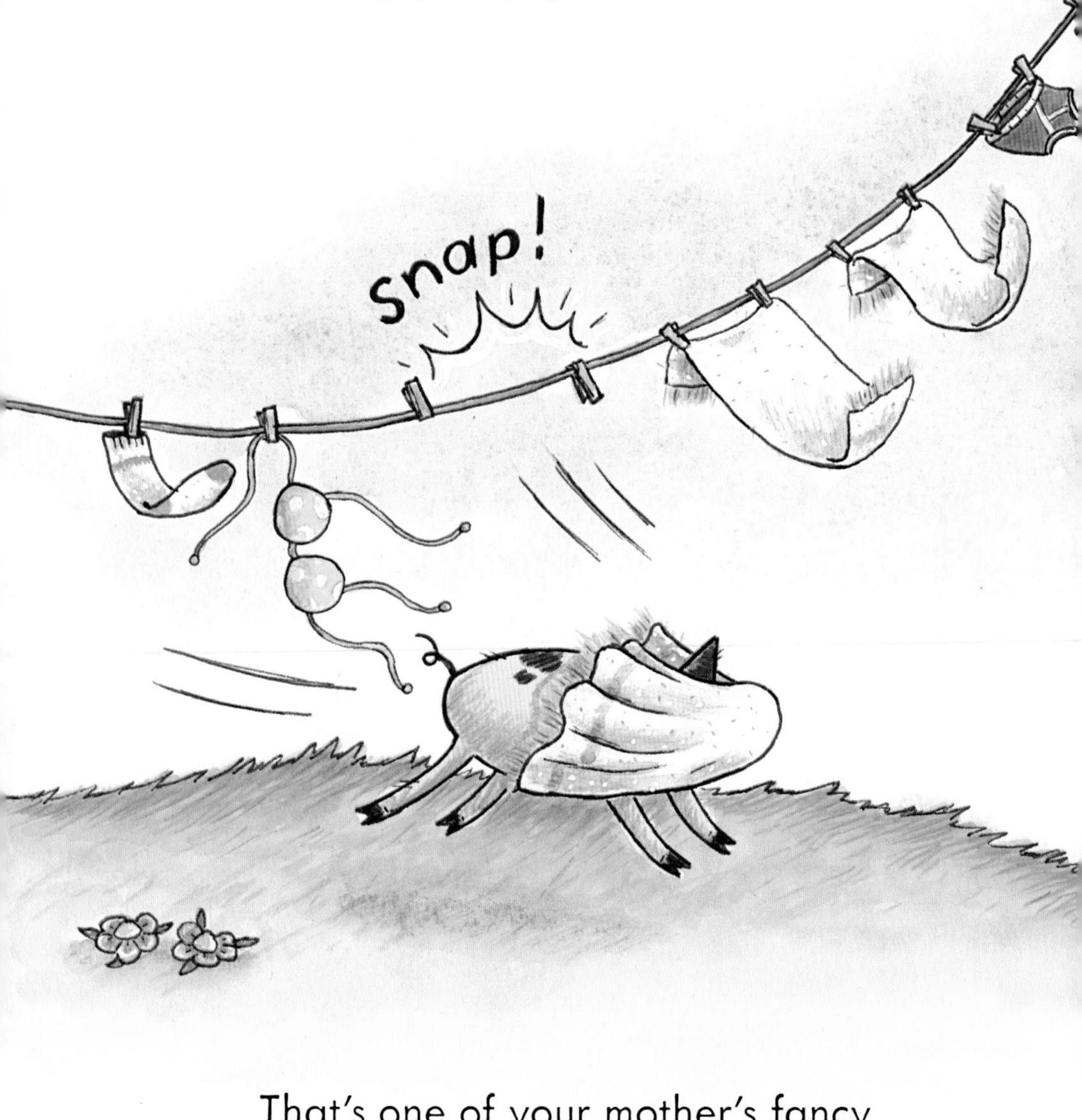
Snap!

That's one of your mother's fancy guest towels—I'm sure she won't mind.

There. Your pig is clean as a whistle!

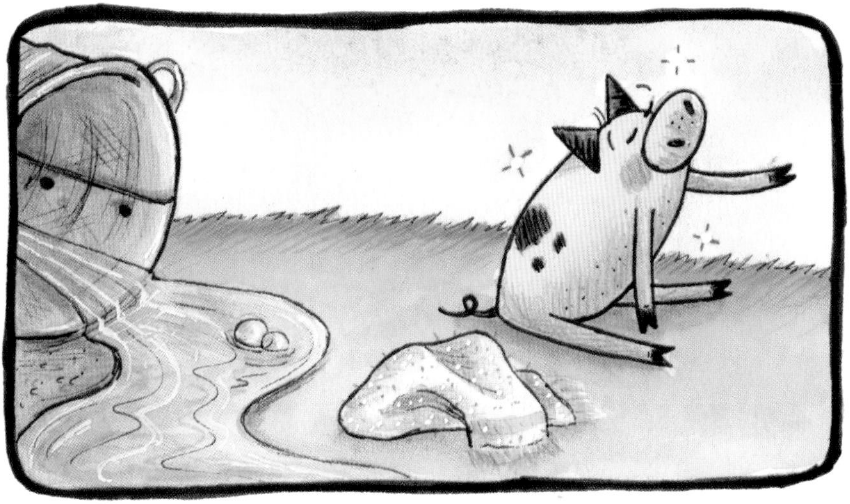

But *you* might need a bath.

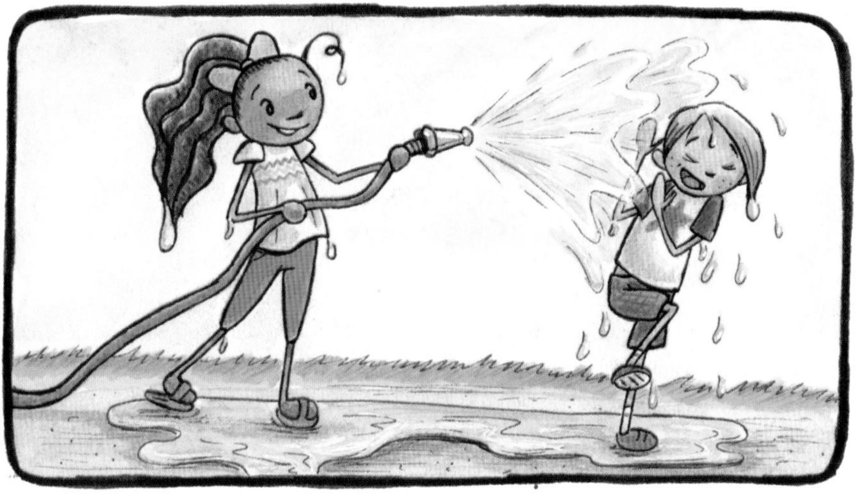

# CHAPTER FOUR

After his bath, your pig will be *super* hungry.
As everyone knows, a hungry pig is
a cranky, misbehaving pig.
Your mother will *never* approve,
so it's CHOW TIME!

Feed your pig

- ☐ bucket
- ☐ trough
- ☐ pig food

You'll need a slop bucket.

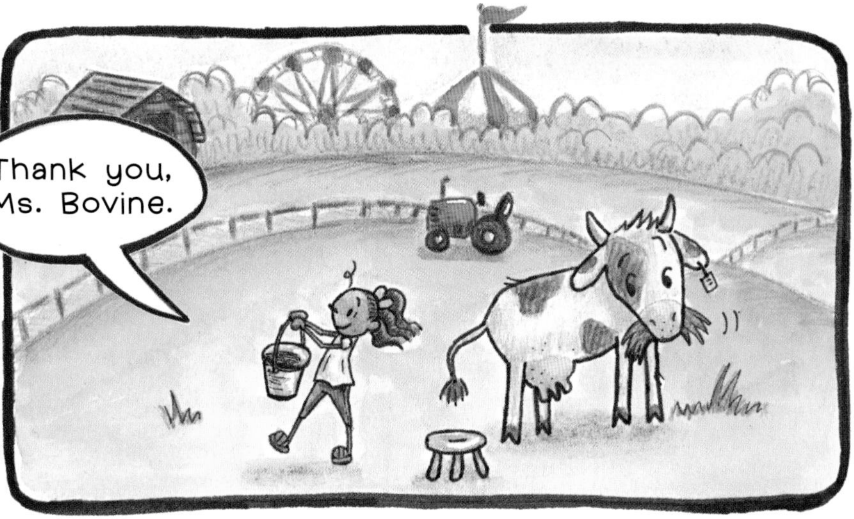
Thank you, Ms. Bovine.

And a trough.

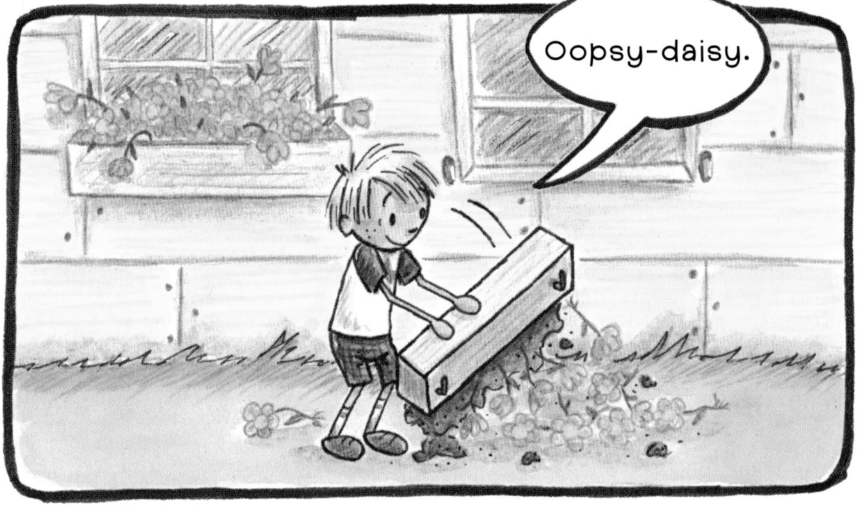
Oopsy-daisy.

And look! Lucky you! There's Mom's garden, with lots of yummy food for pigs.

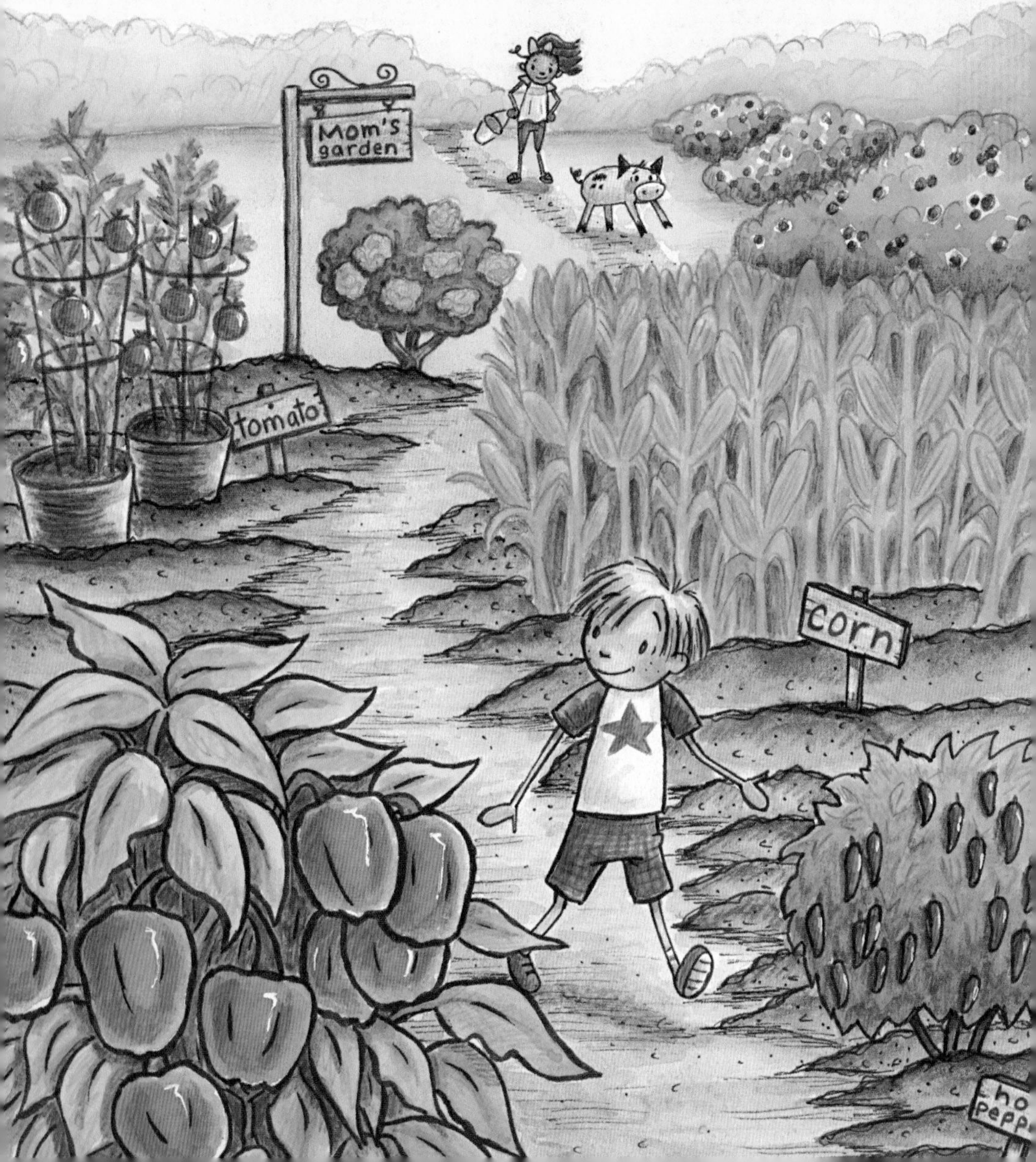
Mom's garden
tomato
corn

Take juicy strawberries,

corn on the cob,

leafy spinach,

and ripe red tomatoes.

Mix it all together.

Lay out Mom's checkered tablecloth.

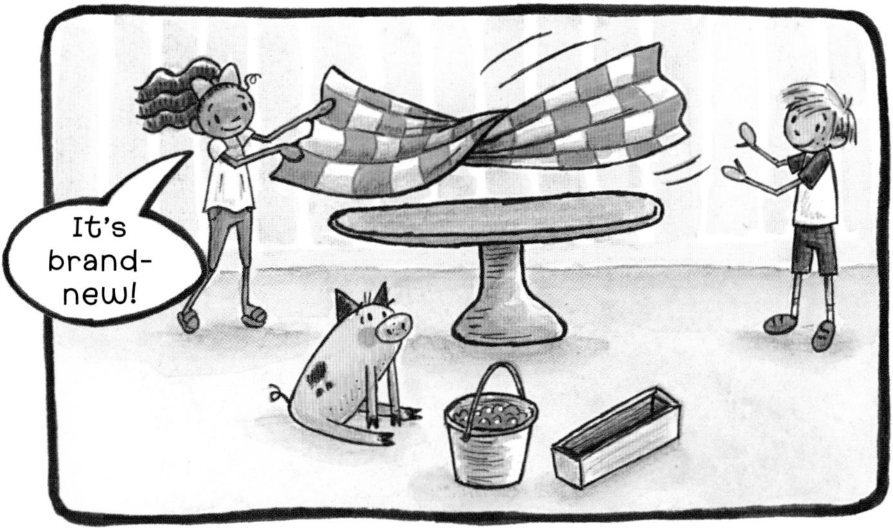
It's brand-new!

Dump the mixture in the trough.

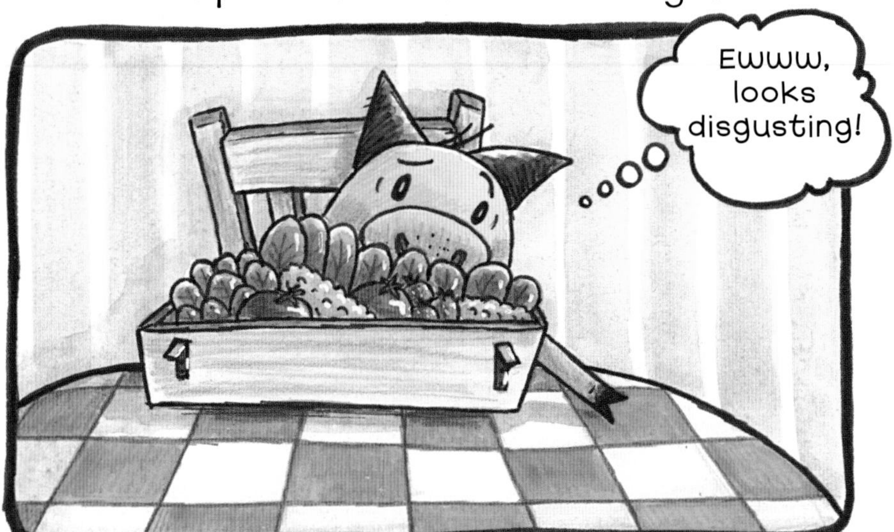
Ewww, looks disgusting!

Lunch is served.

Hmm, it seems as though something else
has tickled your pig's nose . . .

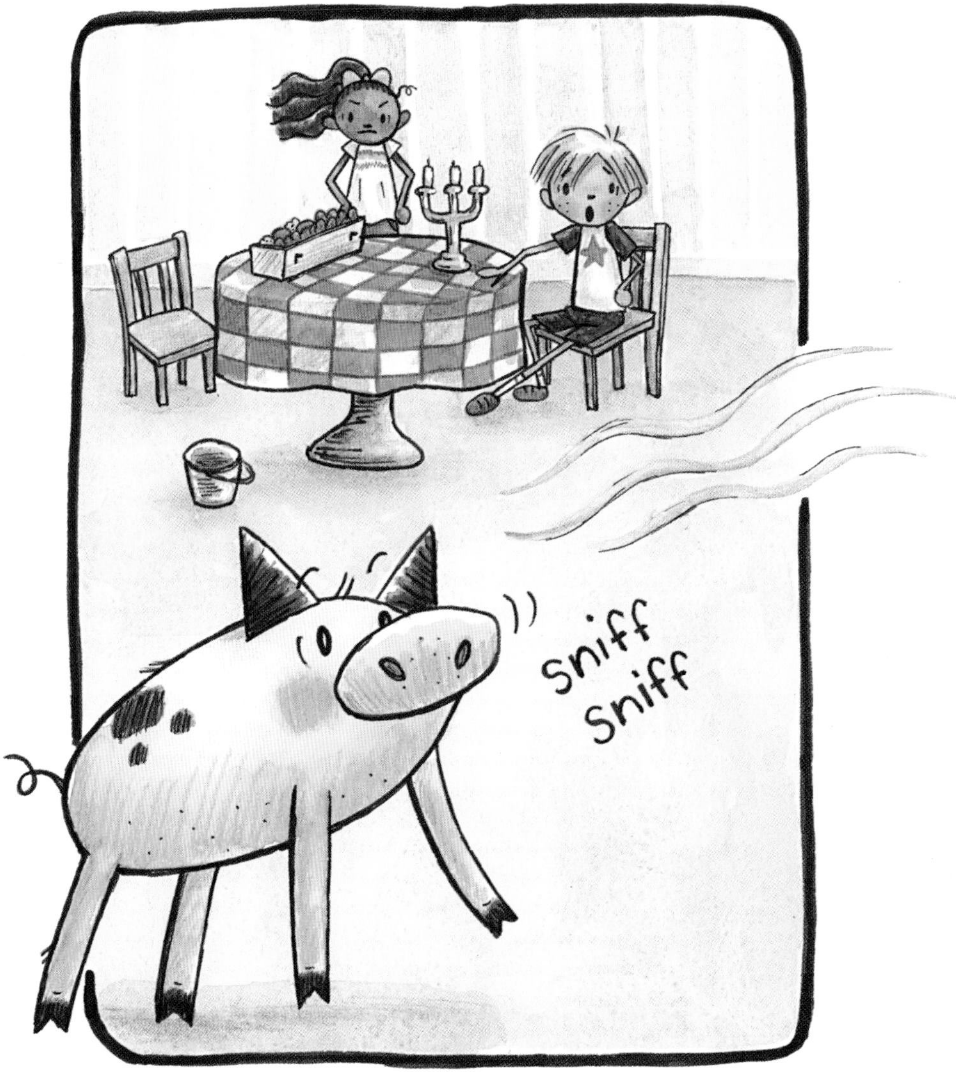
Sniff
Sniff

stale jelly doughnuts!

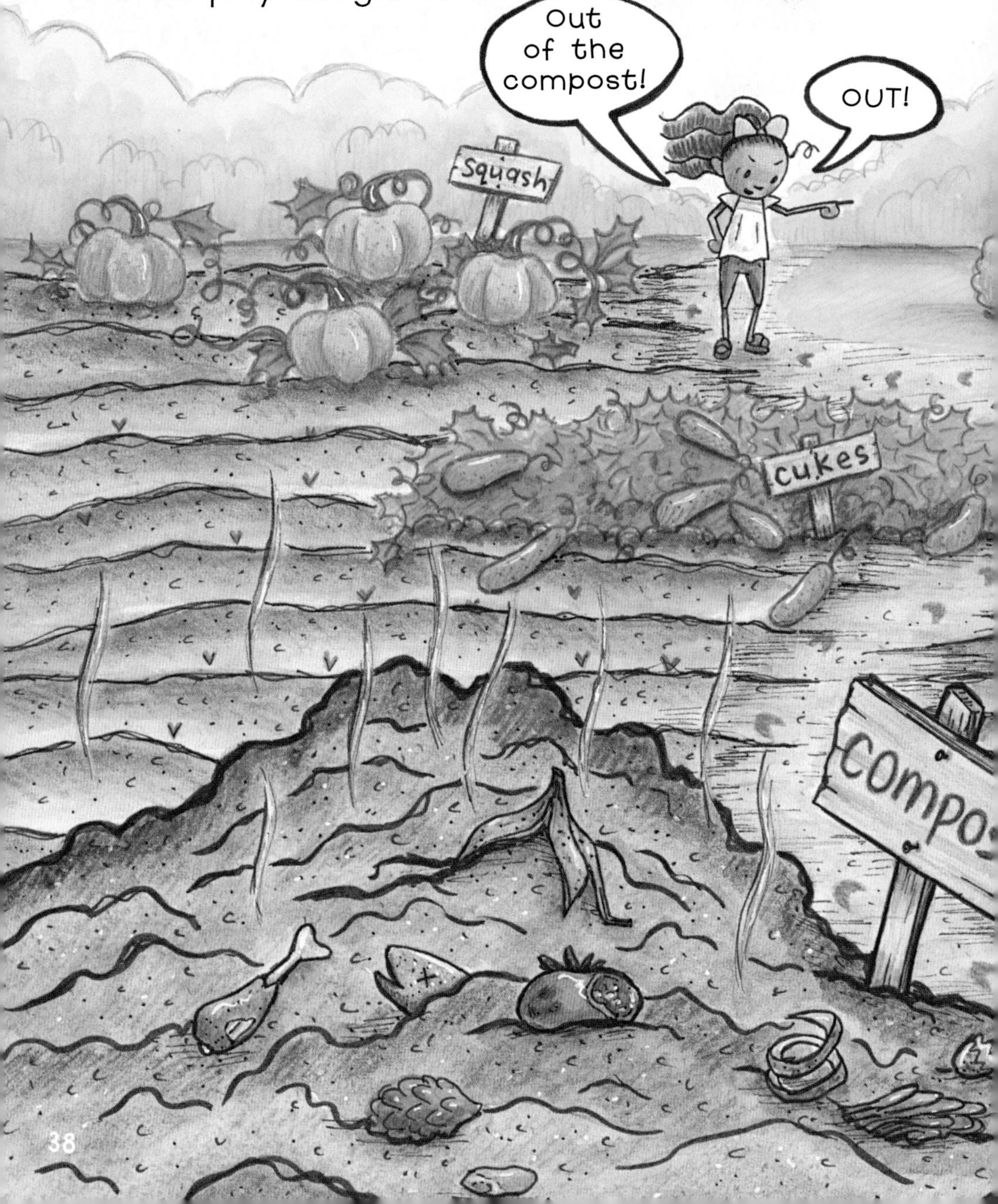
Out of the compost!
OUT!
Squash
cukes
COMPO

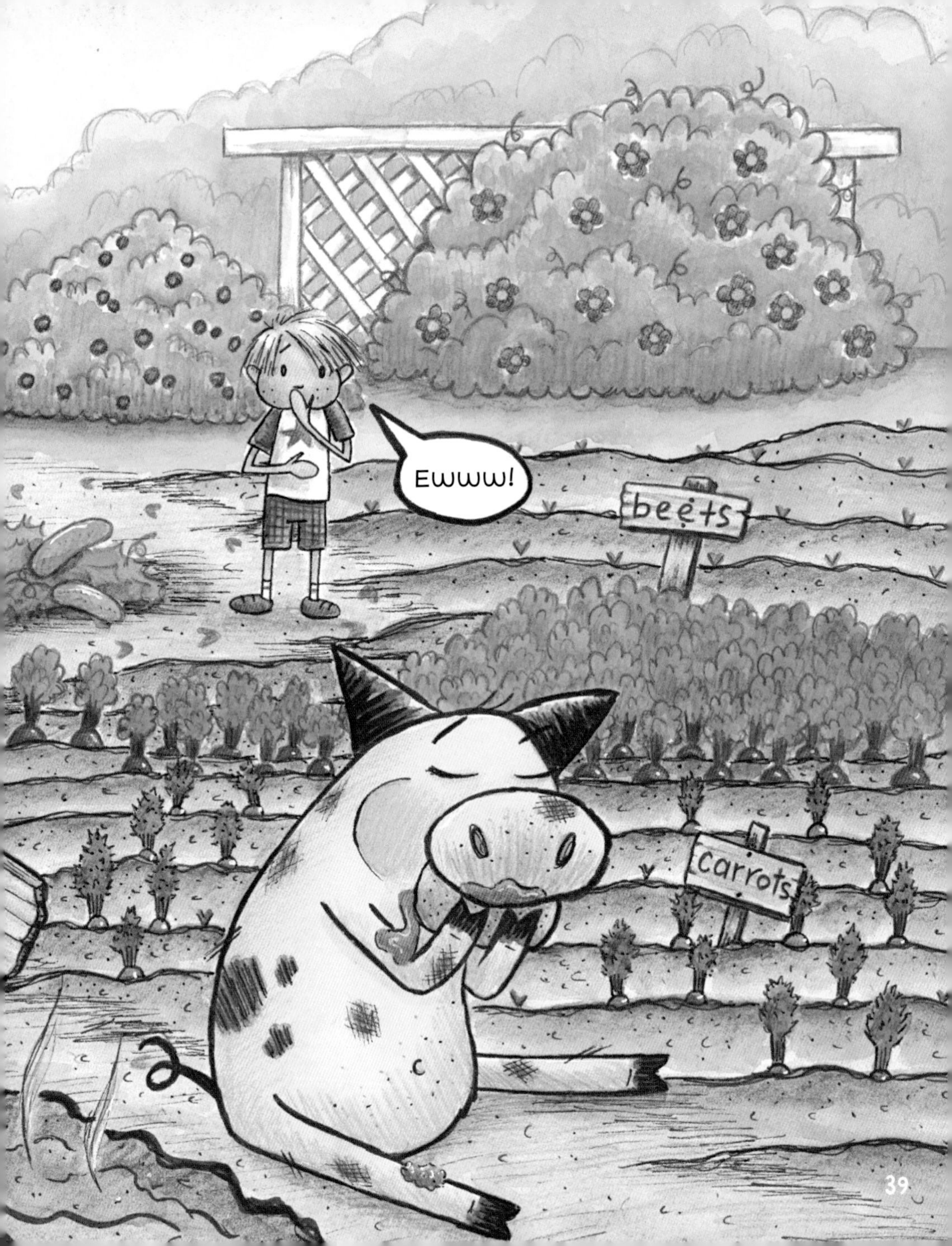
Ewww!
beets
carrots

Well, it's back to the second item on your list:
You have to bathe your pig all over again.

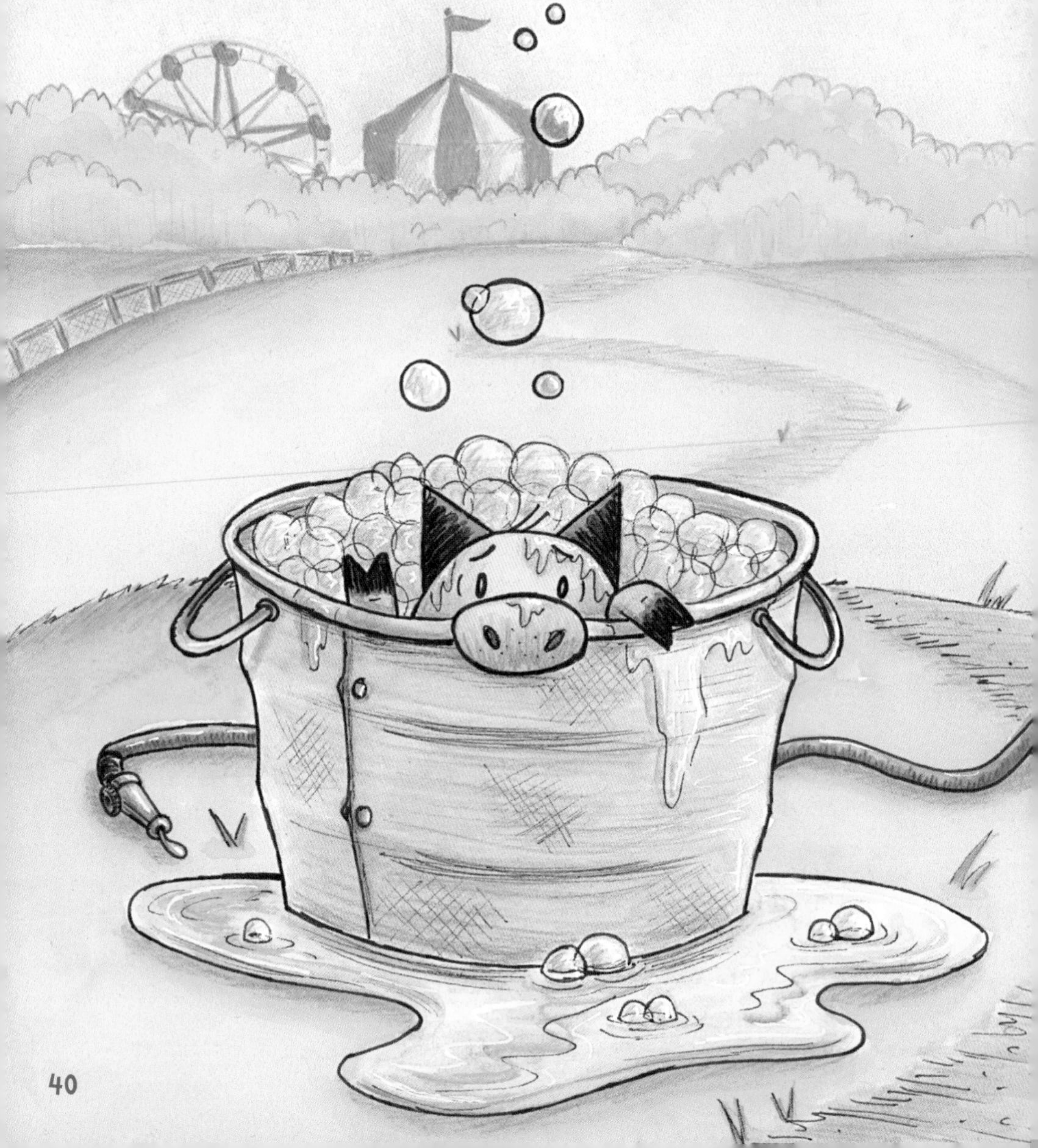

# CHAPTER FIVE

Now that you've:

☑ picked your pig,

☑ cleaned your pig,

☑ fed your pig,

☑ and cleaned your pig again,

it's time to move on to the fun part:

# TRICKS!

When you were younger, you might have learned to

juggle,

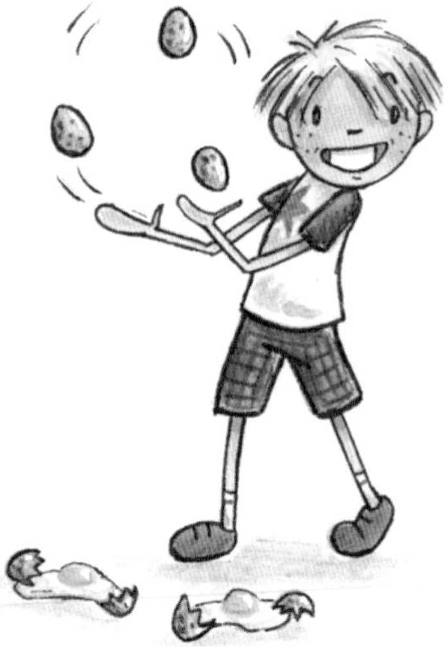

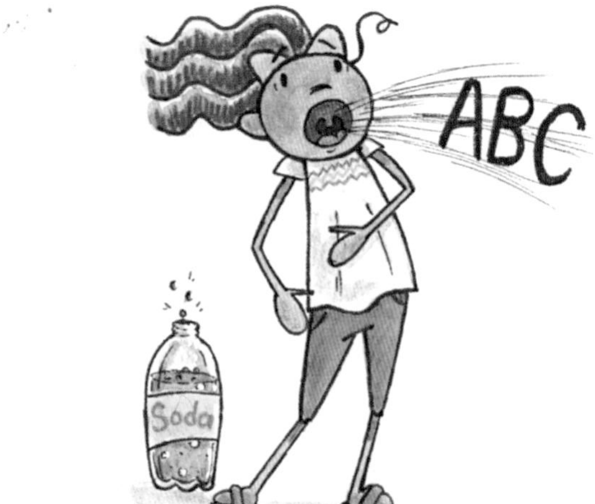
ABC
Soda

burp the alphabet,

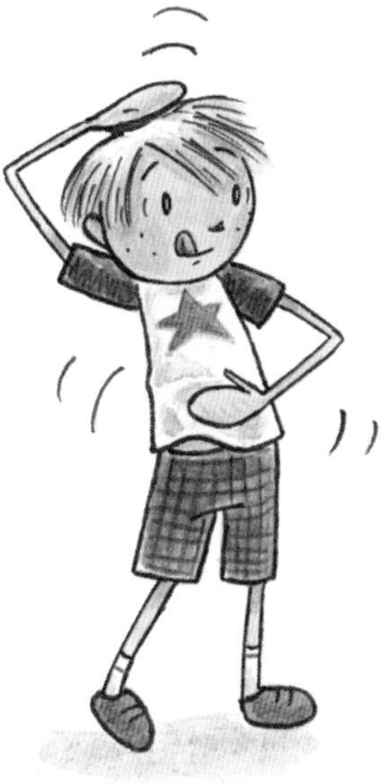

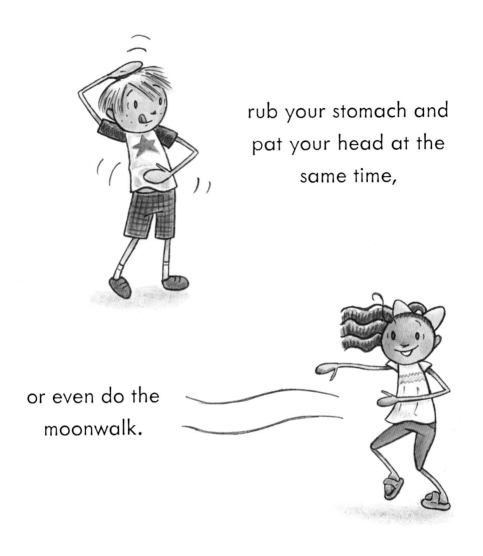

rub your stomach and pat your head at the same time,

or even do the moonwalk.

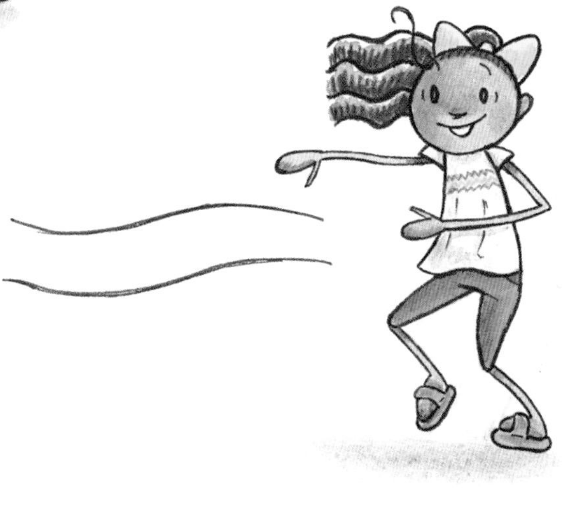

Your mom was *so* proud.
I'm positive if your pig learns even a few tricks, your mom will have to say yes!

Ask Snowflake
to juggle,

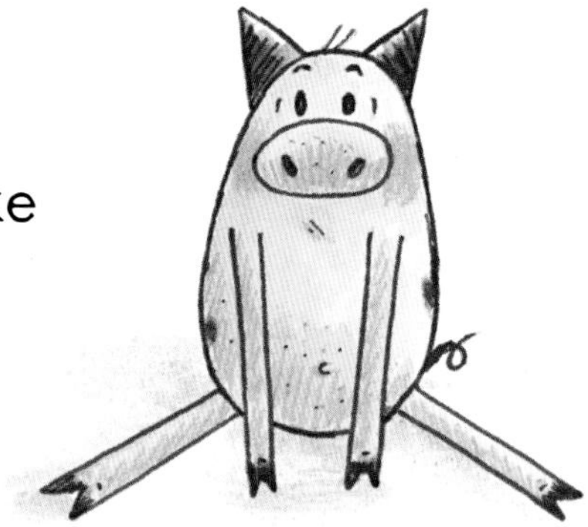

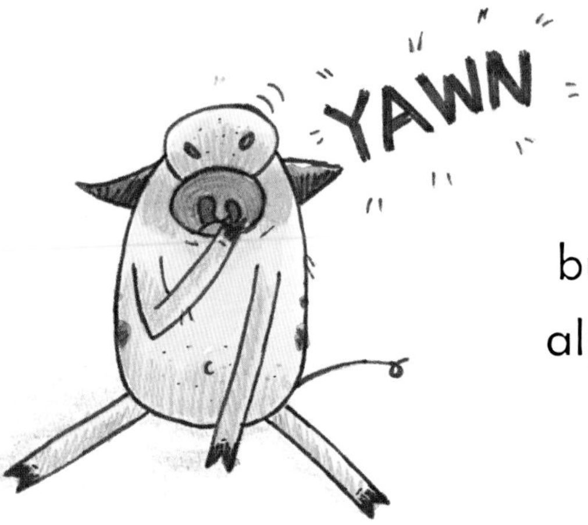
YAWN

burp the
alphabet,

rub his stomach
and pat his head
at the same time,

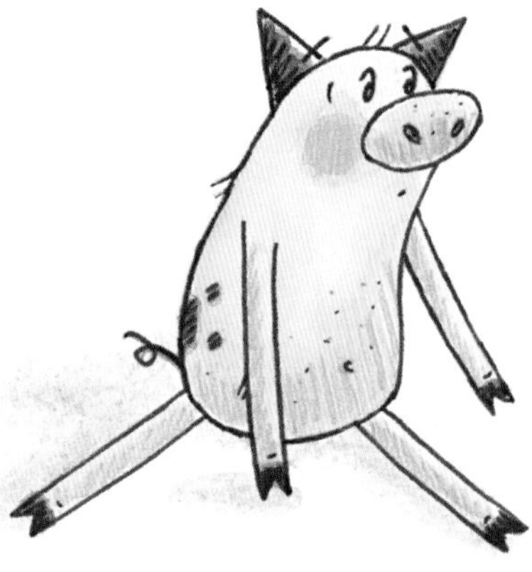

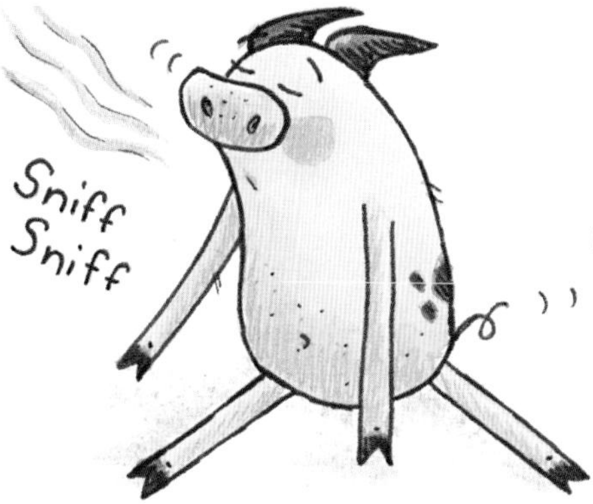
Sniff
Sniff

or do the moonwalk.

Well, at least there's one trick Snowflake has learned. . . .

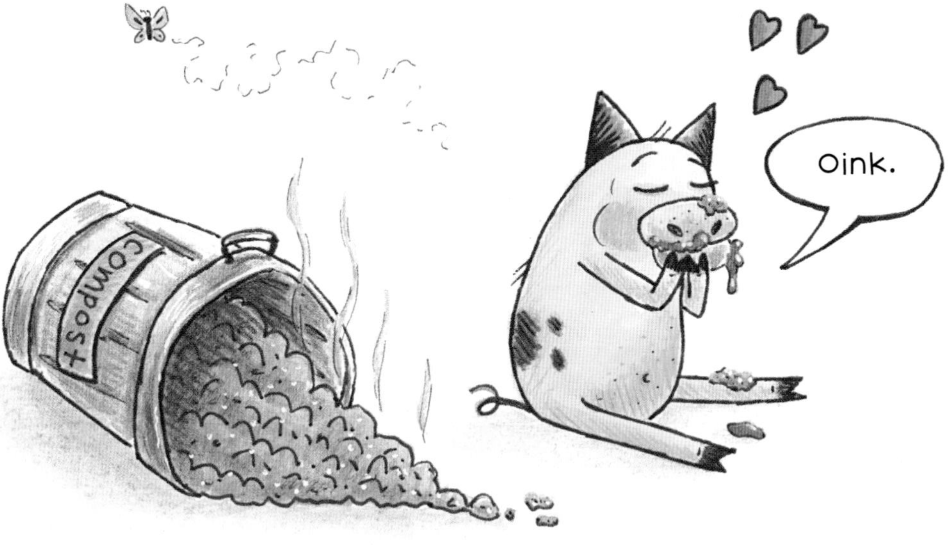
Oink.
COMPOST

# CHAPTER SIX

It may appear that your scheme isn't
exactly working.

Maybe you should take Snowflake to the
county fair. He's blue-ribbon material!

Your mom can't say no to a prizewinning pig!
(Remember, her petunias won the
first-place prize.)

Golden Trowel Award

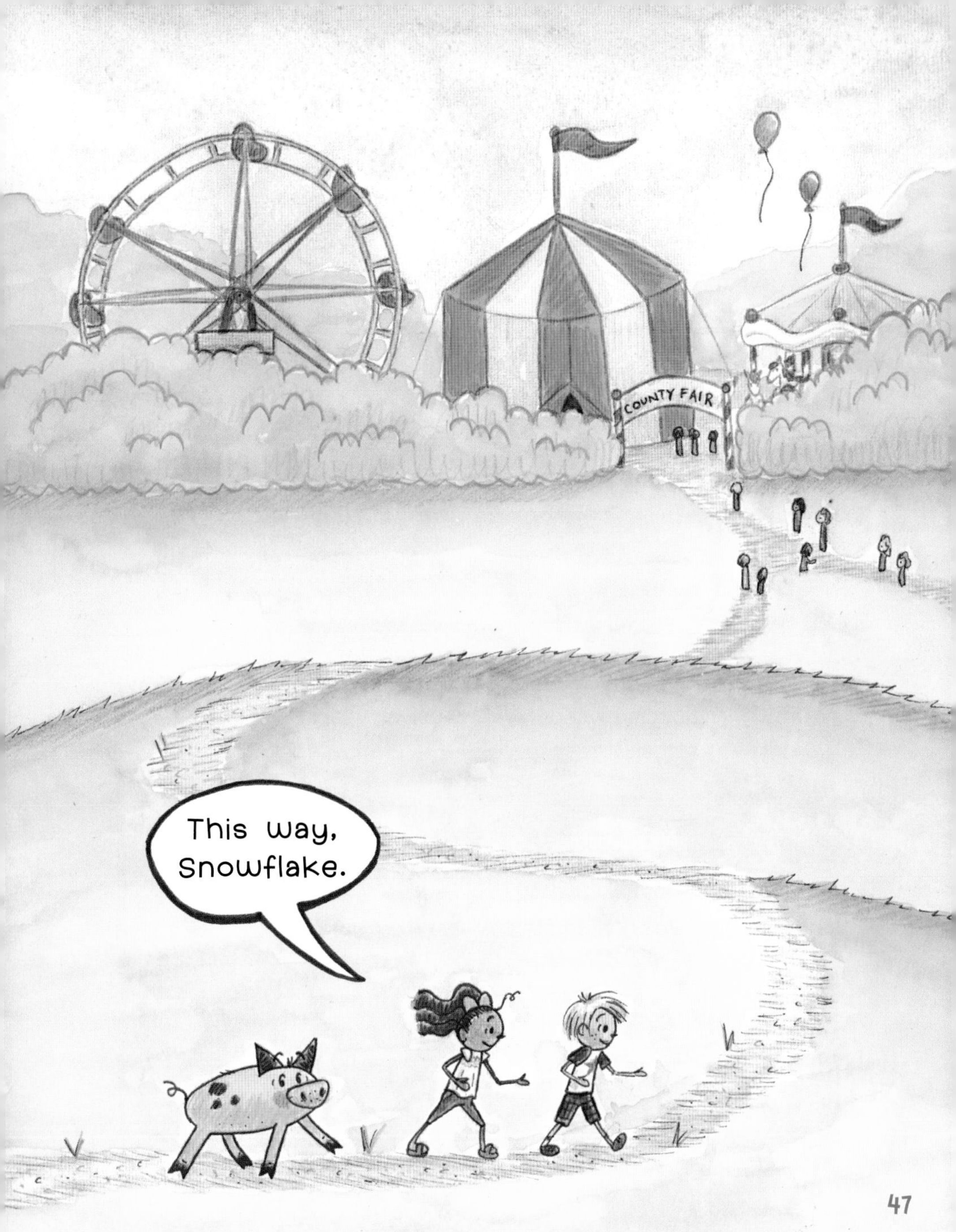
COUNTY FAIR
This way, Snowflake.

Snowflake is sure to be a front-runner in the pie-eating contest.

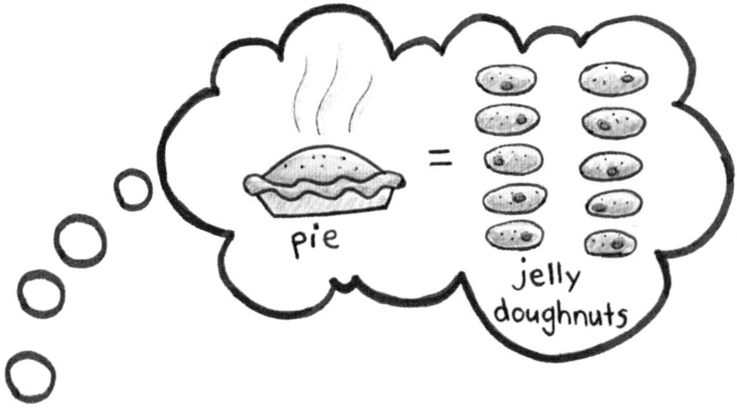
pie
=
jelly doughnuts

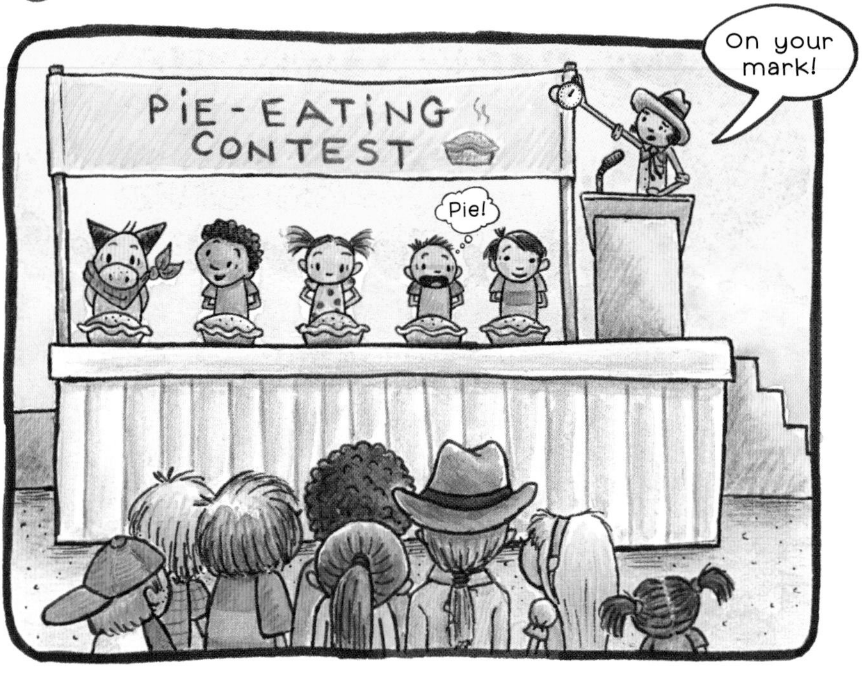
On your mark!
PIE-EATING CONTEST
Pie!

But wait a minute! Where are *you* going?

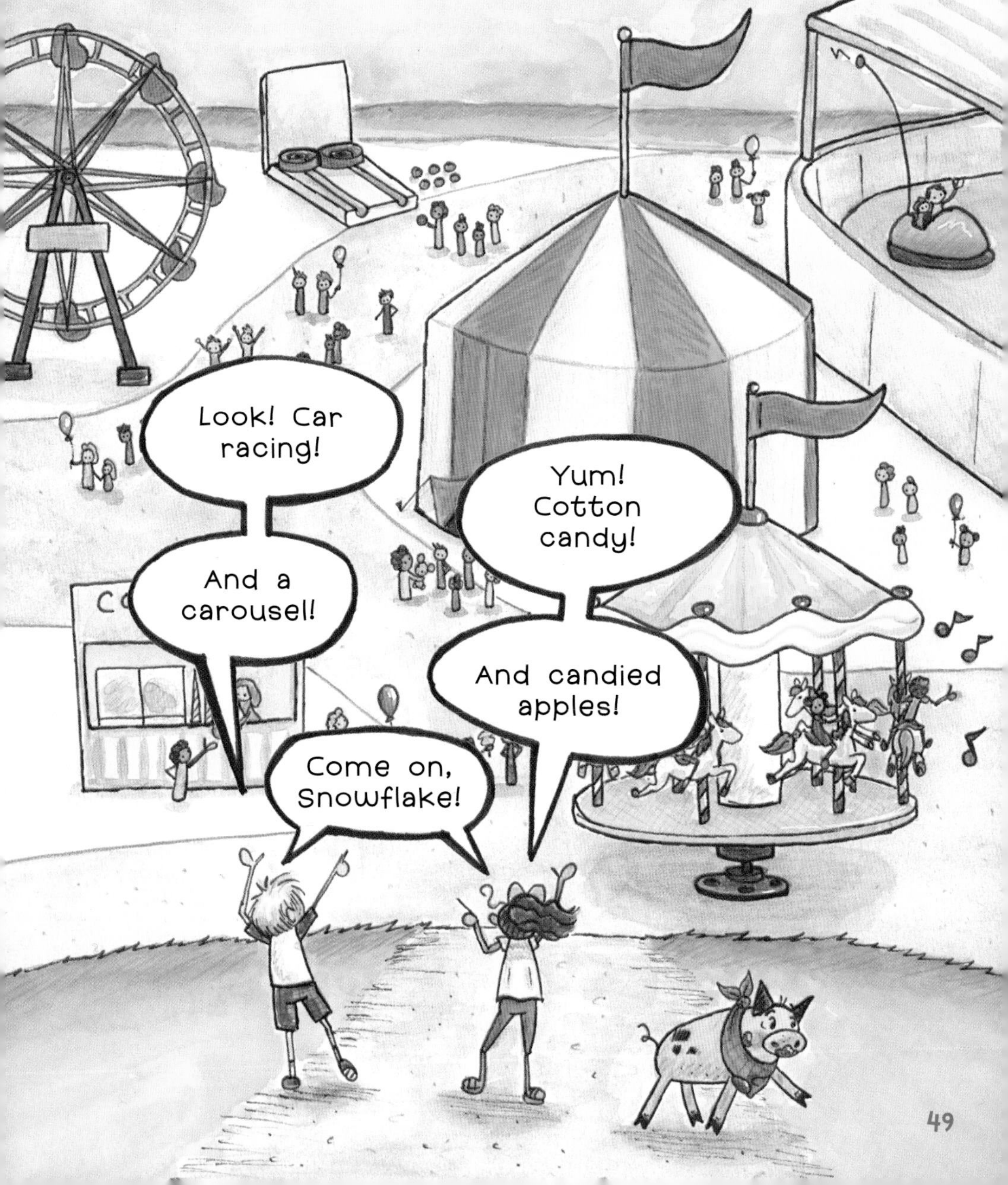
Look! Car racing!
And a carousel!
Yum! Cotton candy!
And candied apples!
Come on, Snowflake!

County fairs are fun for everyone.

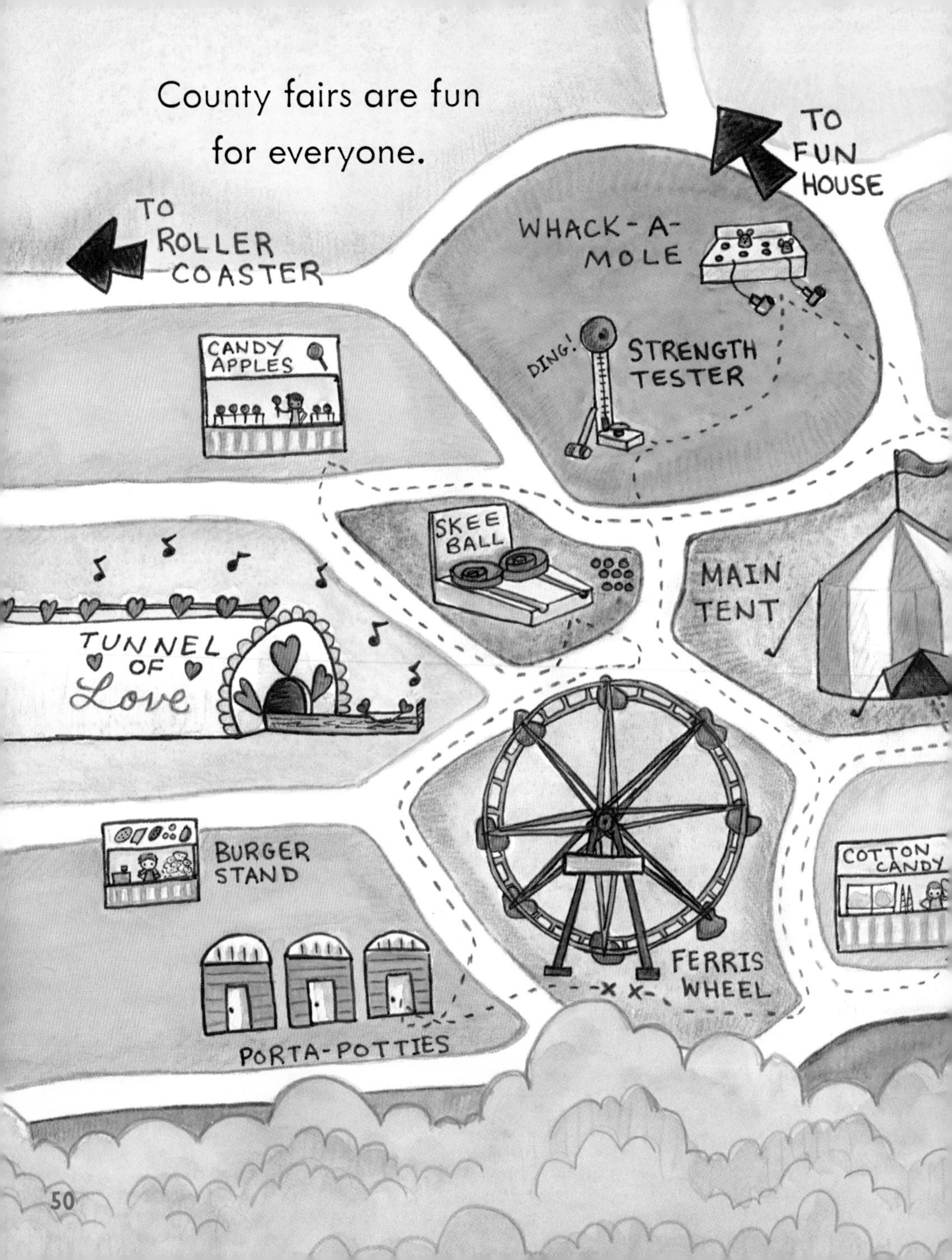
TO ROLLER COASTER
TO FUN HOUSE
WHACK-A-MOLE
CANDY APPLES
DING!
STRENGTH TESTER
SKEE BALL
MAIN TENT
TUNNEL OF Love
BURGER STAND
COTTON CANDY
FERRIS WHEEL
PORTA-POTTIES

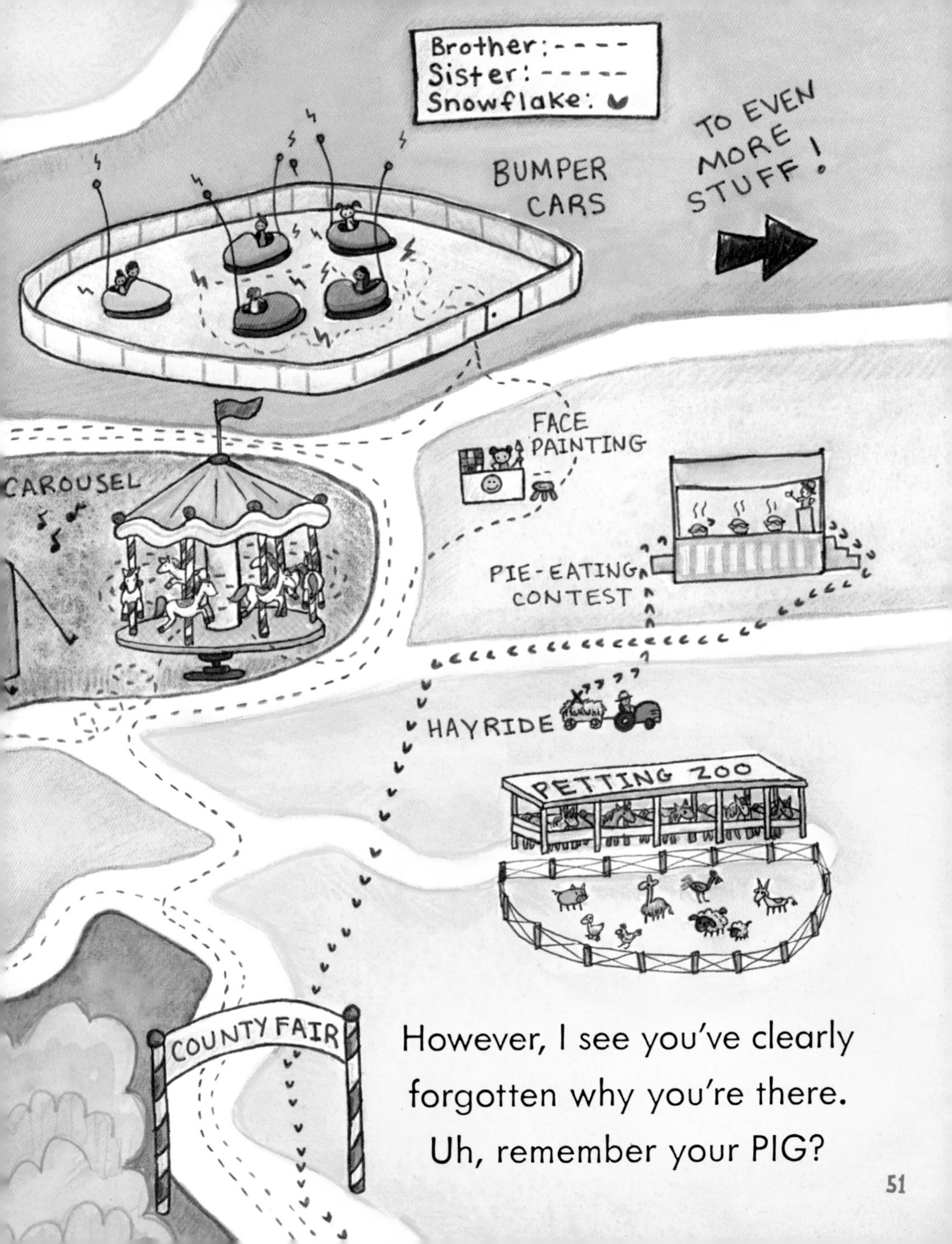
Brother: ----
Sister: -----
Snowflake:
BUMPER CARS
TO EVEN MORE STUFF!
FACE PAINTING
CAROUSEL
PIE-EATING CONTEST
HAYRIDE
PETTING ZOO
COUNTY FAIR

However, I see you've clearly forgotten why you're there. Uh, remember your PIG?

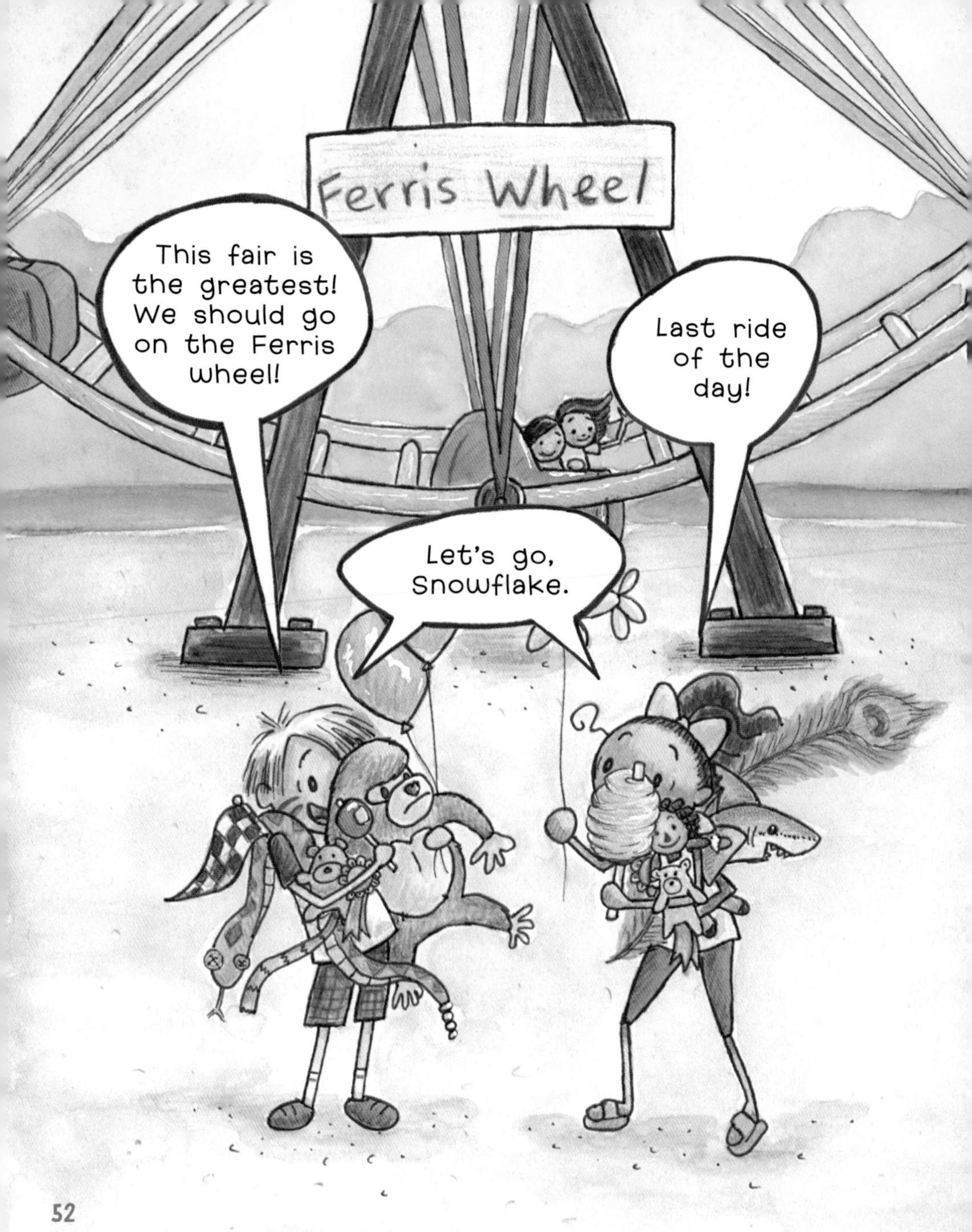
Ferris Wheel
This fair is the greatest! We should go on the Ferris wheel!
Last ride of the day!
Let's go, Snowflake.

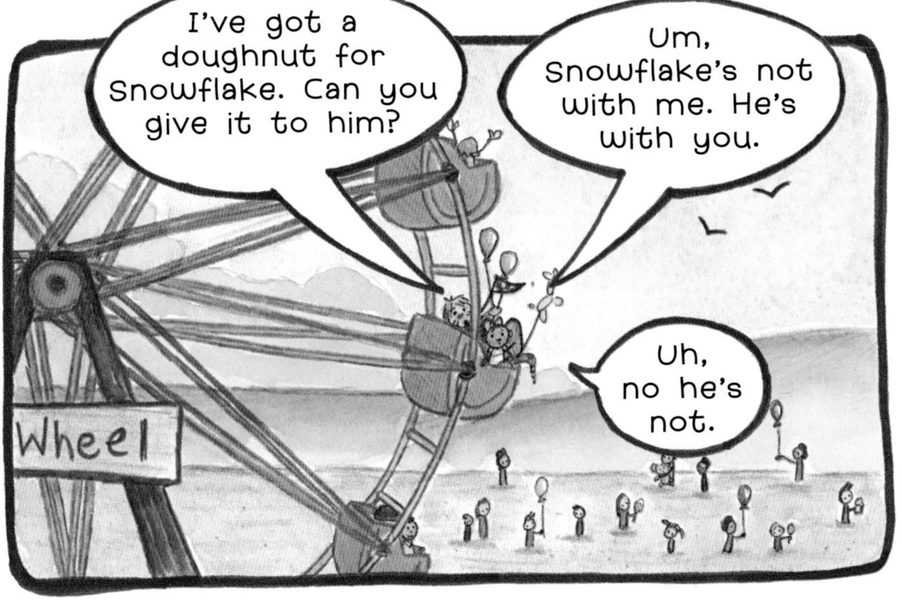
I've got a doughnut for Snowflake. Can you give it to him?
Um, Snowflake's not with me. He's with you.
Uh, no he's not.
Wheel

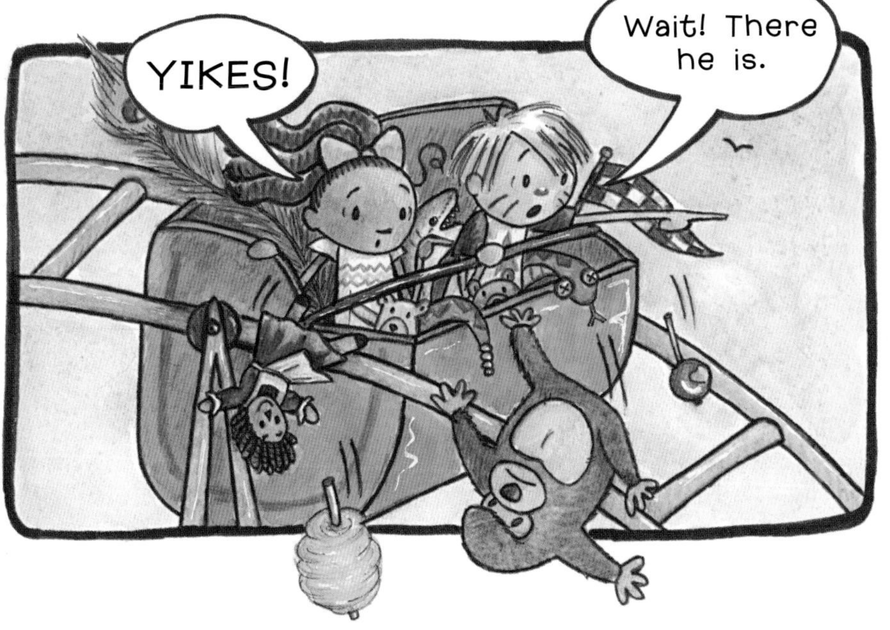
YIKES!
Wait! There he is.

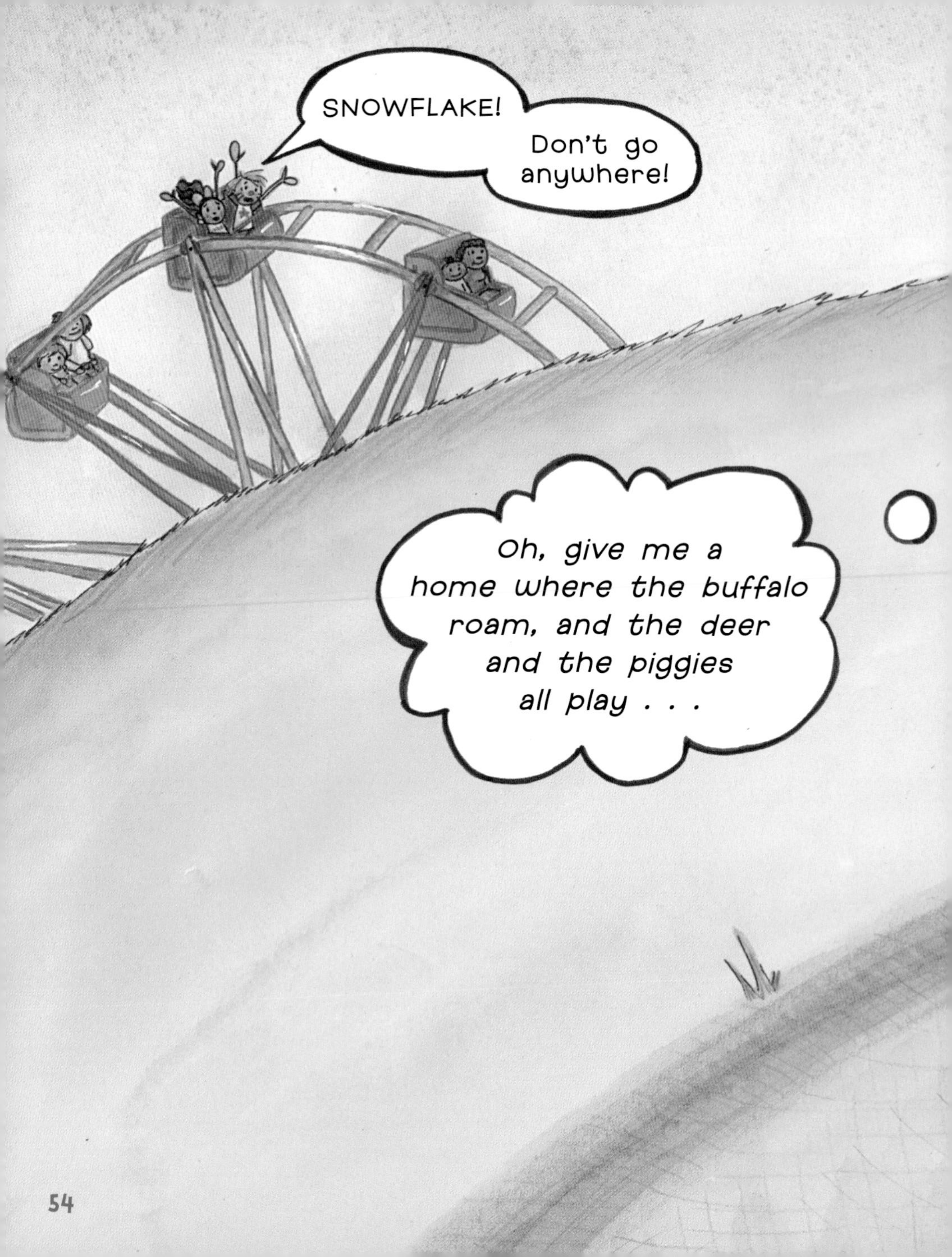
SNOWFLAKE!
Don't go anywhere!
Oh, give me a home where the buffalo roam, and the deer and the piggies all play . . .

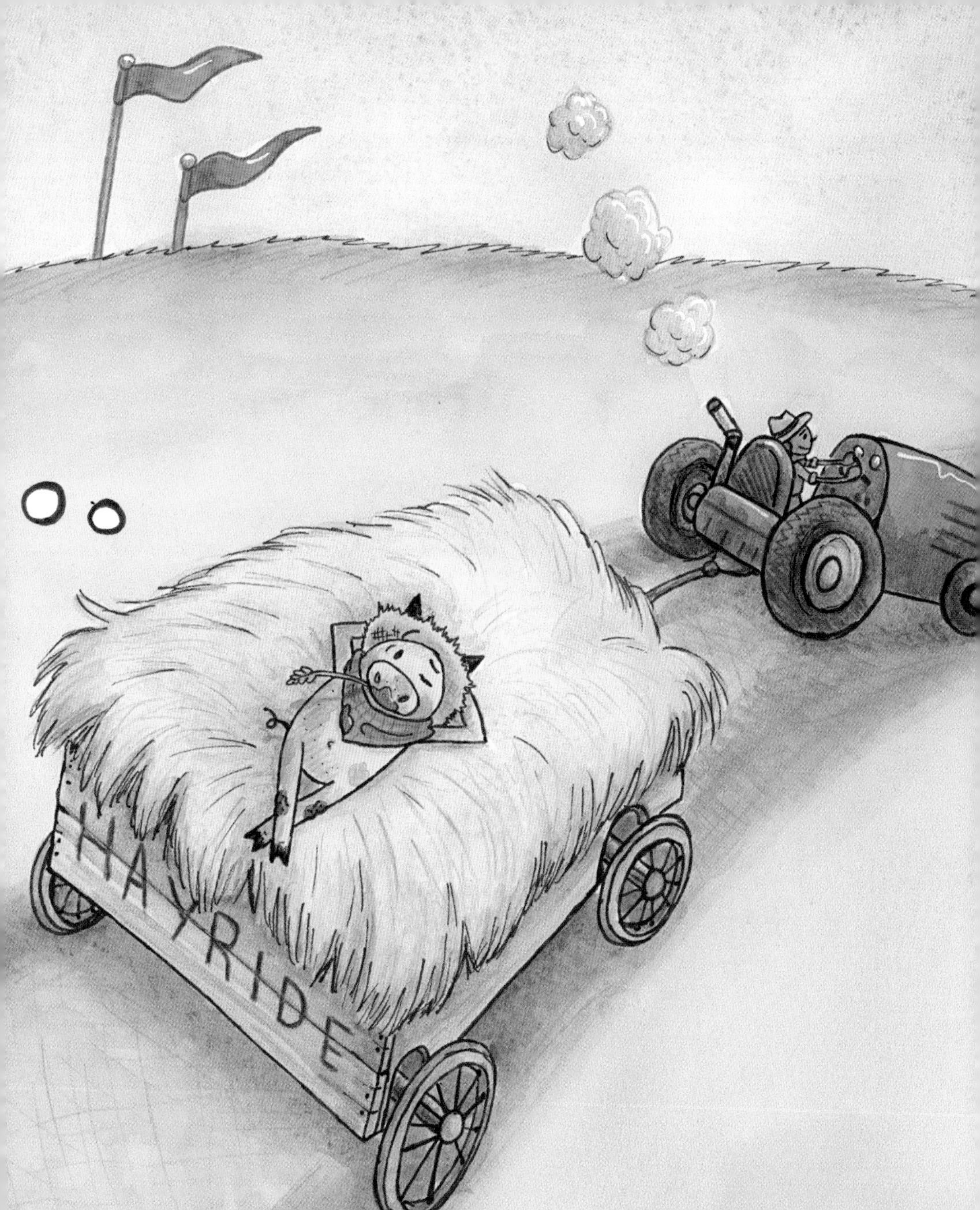
HAYRIDE

Once the Ferris wheel stops, you and your brother jump out and fetch your pig.

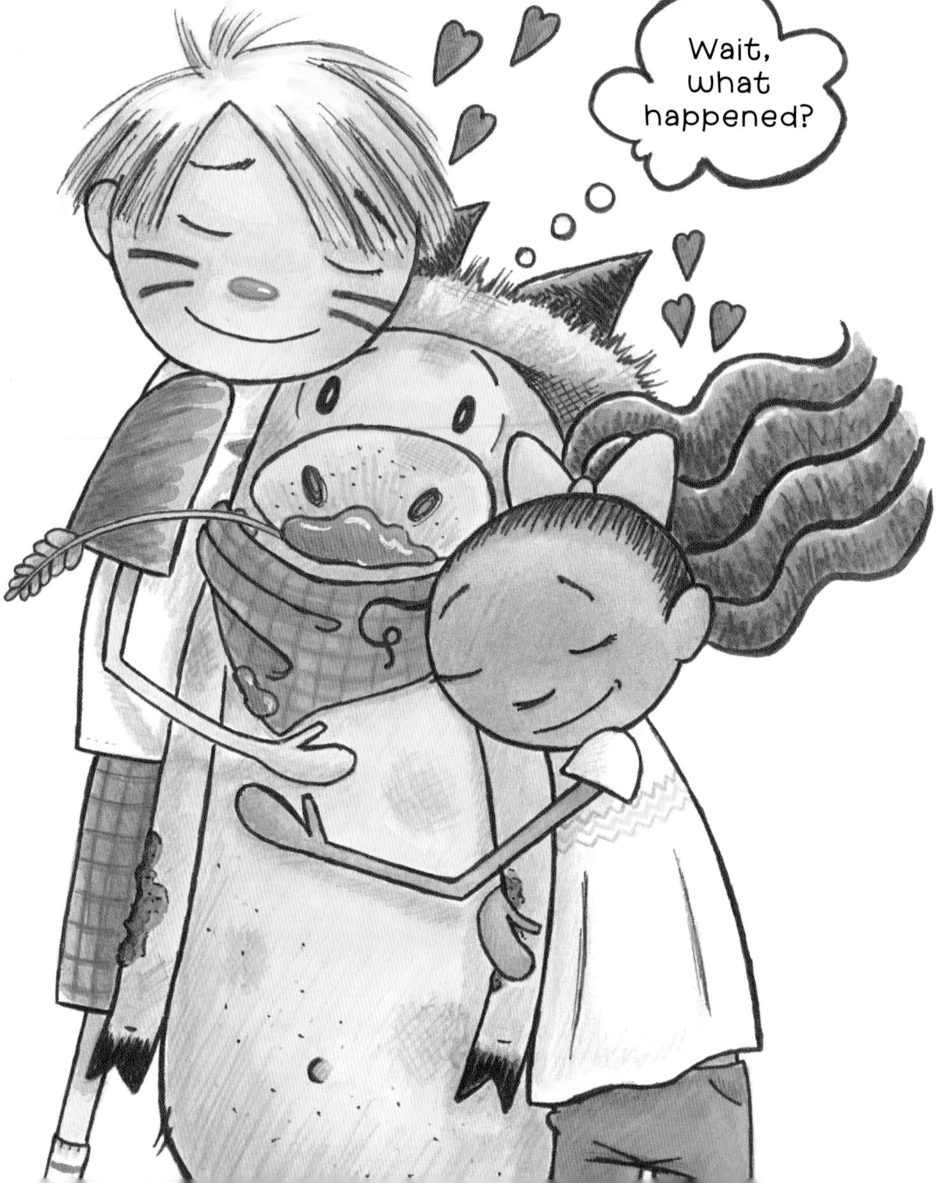
Wait, what happened?

So maybe Snowflake is never clean, eats from the garbage, and can't do tricks.

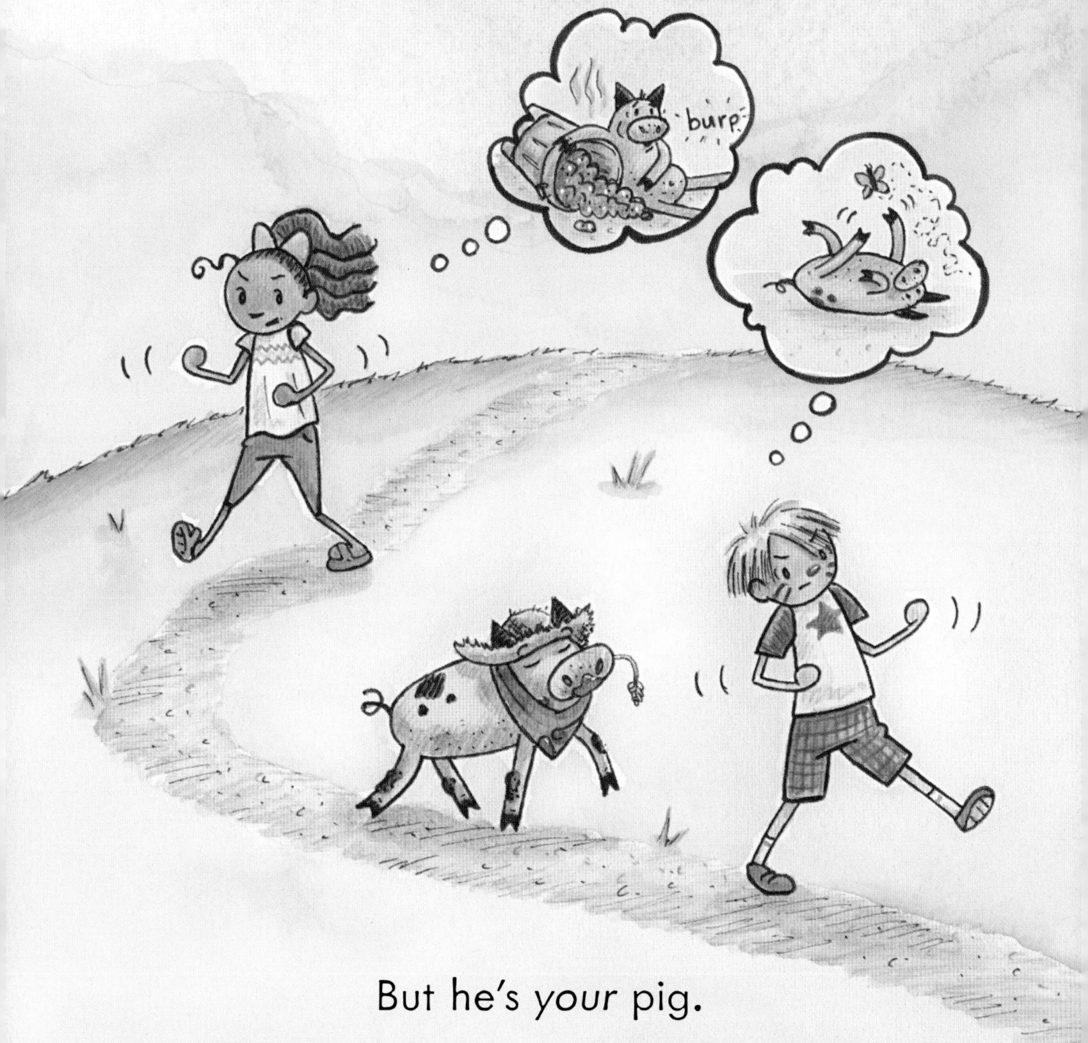
burp

But he's *your* pig.

Now is as good a time as any to head home . . .

to introduce Snowflake to your mother.

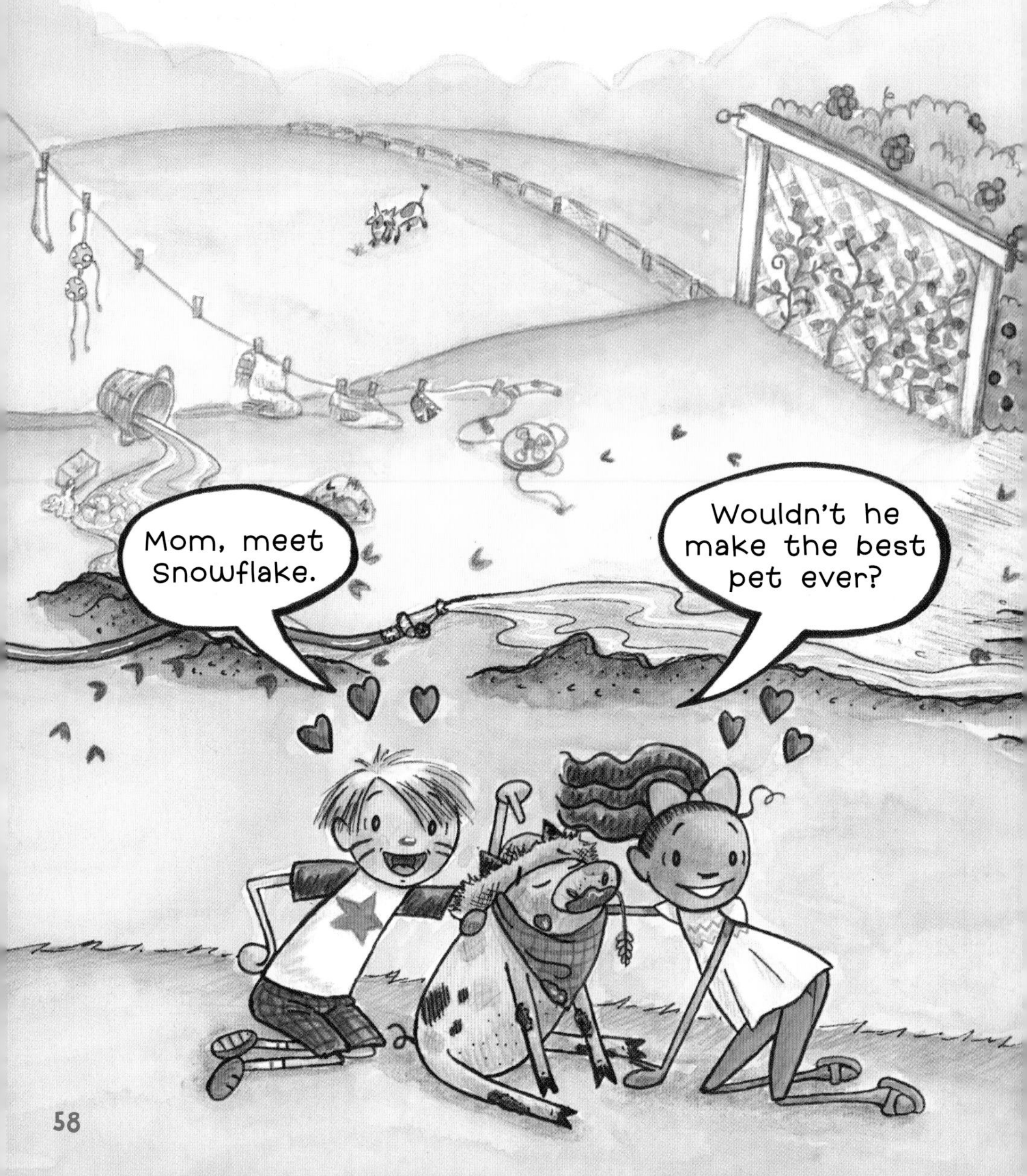
Mom, meet Snowflake.
Wouldn't he make the best pet ever?

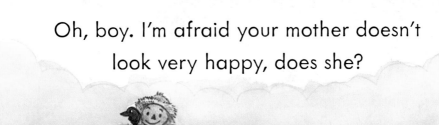

Oh, boy. I'm afraid your mother doesn't look very happy, does she?

But suddenly Snowflake takes off into the garden!
Get out of here, you pesky crows!

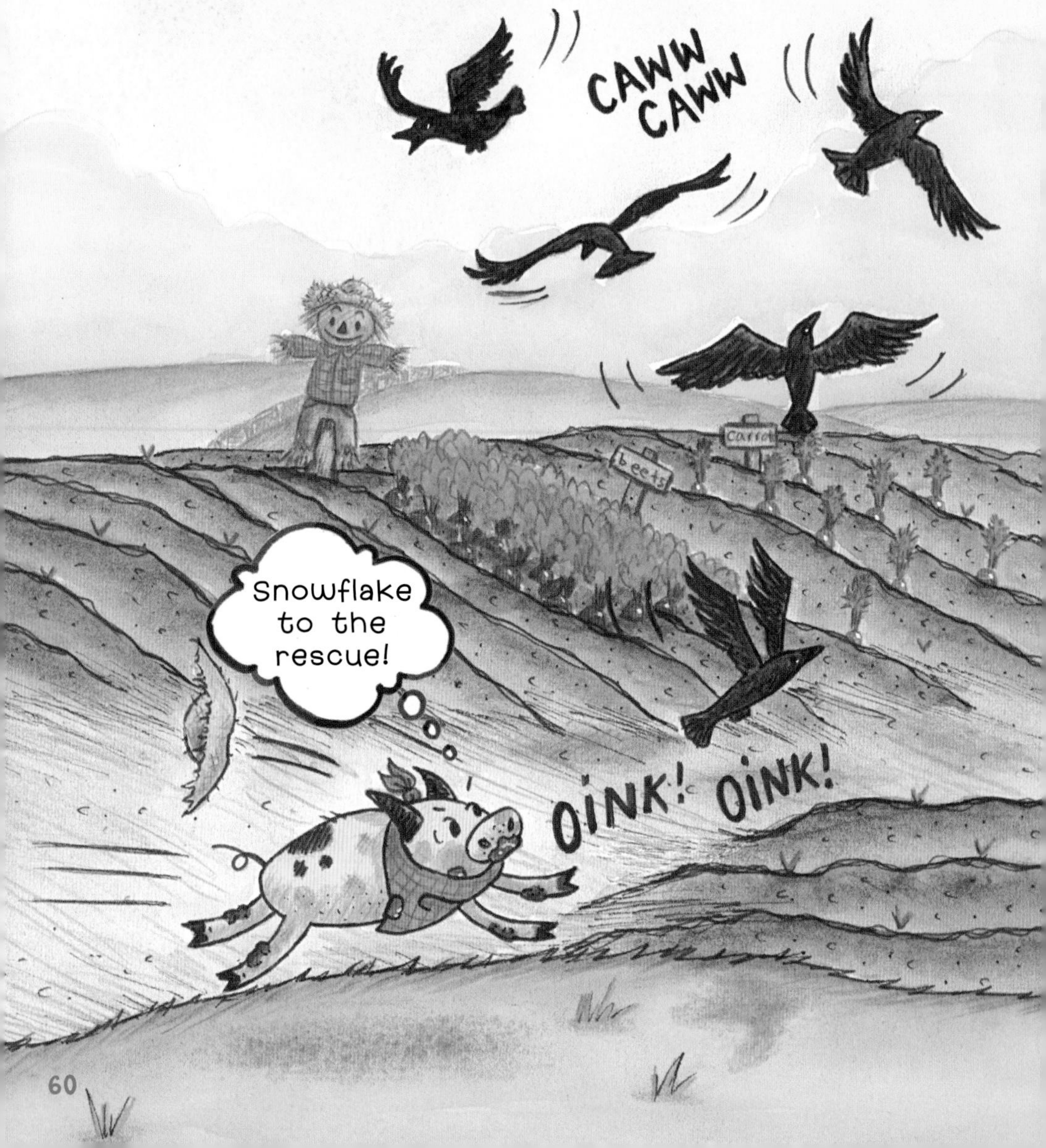
CAWW CAWW
beets
Carrot
Snowflake to the rescue!
OINK! OINK!

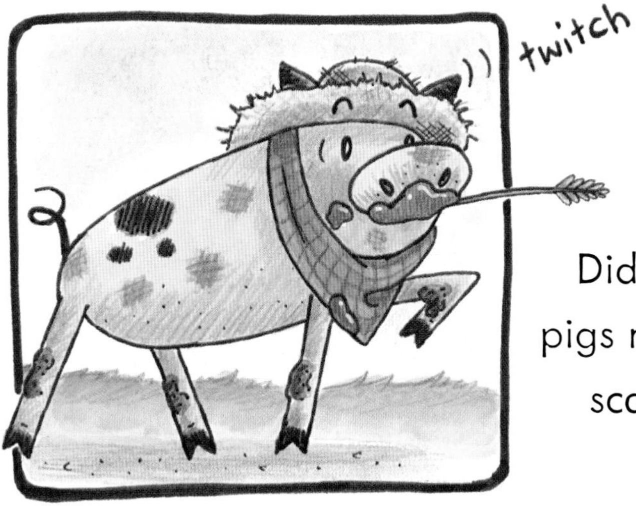
twitch

Did I mention pigs make terrific scarecrows?

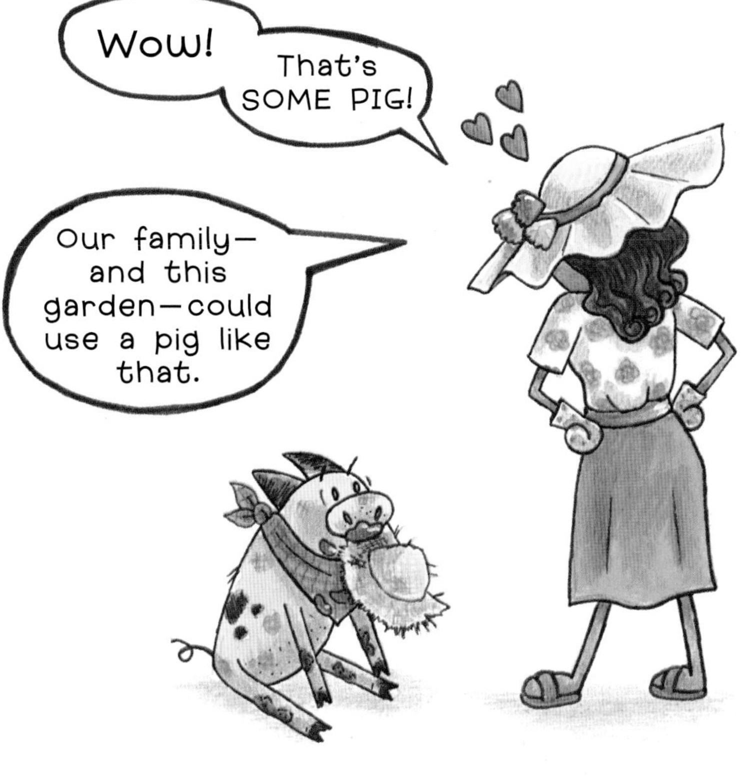
Wow!
That's SOME PIG!
Our family—and this garden—could use a pig like that.

Did you hear that, you little schemers?
Mom said yes! Snowflake is all yours.

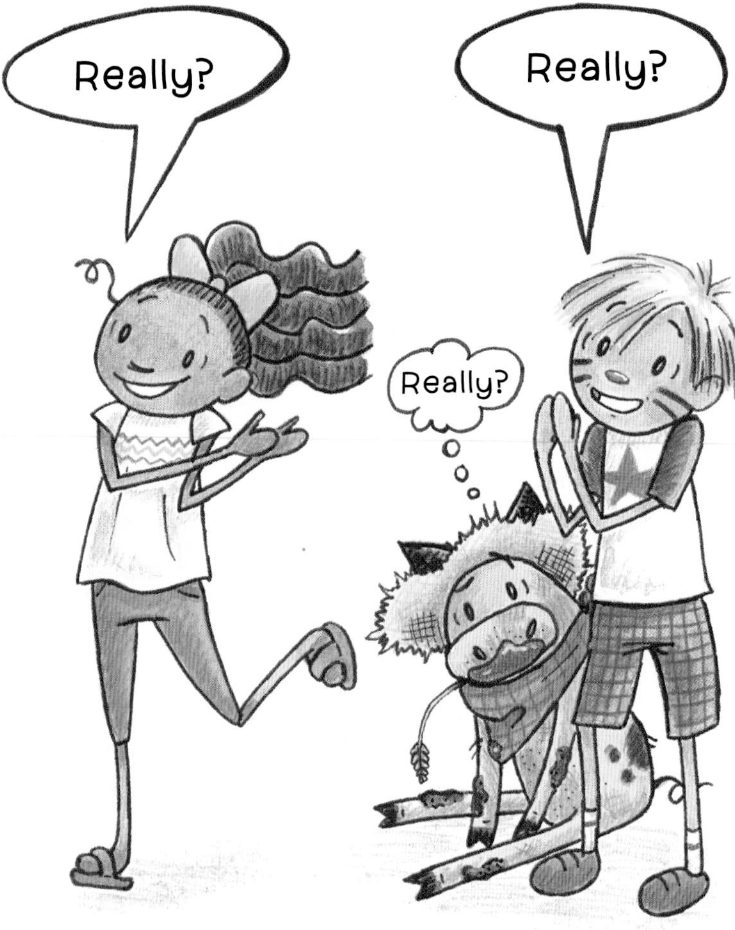
Really?
Really?
Really?

YAHOO!

How are you going to celebrate?

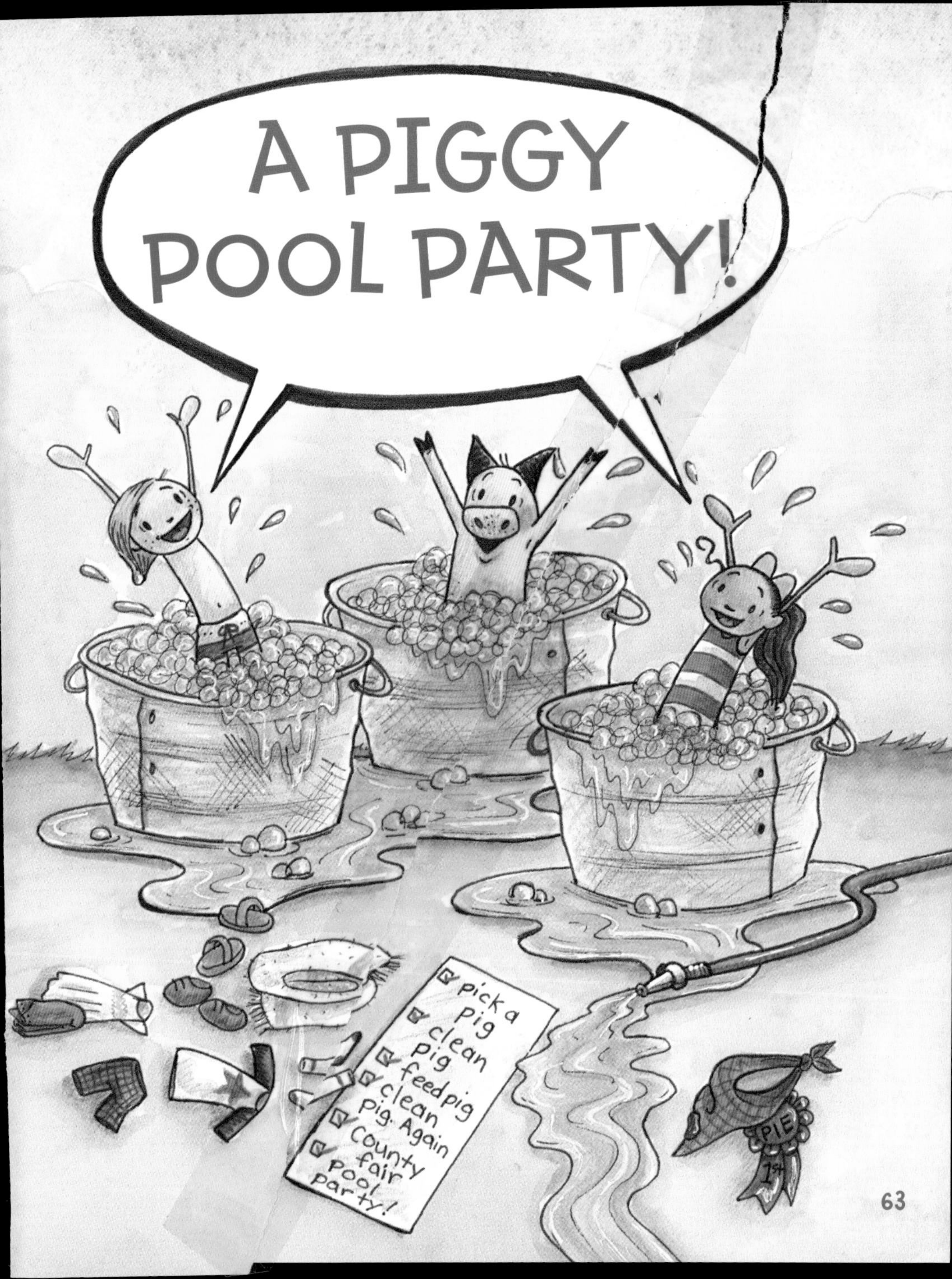
A PIGGY POOL PARTY!
pick a pig
clean pig
feed pig
clean pig. Again
County fair
Pool party!
PIE
1st